I hurried outside. Ma had got the mules out of harness and into the stalls. She was up in the haymow pitching down some hay for them.

"I'll do that, Ma. You go on in and tend to Pa."

She put the pitchfork down and clambered down the haymow ladder. "What did he want to tell you?"

"He made me promise not to run off to fight. He made me promise to stay here and help with things."

"I figured that was it," she said. "Did you promise?"

"Yes."

"I'm glad," she said. She put her arms on my shoulders and looked me square in the face, for we were about the same height. "It'd kill me to lose another one, Johnny."

James Lincoln Collier is the coauthor, with his brother, Christopher, of *My Brother Sam Is Dead*, a Newbery Honor Book. They have also written *Jump Ship to Freedom*, *War Comes to Willy Freeman*, *Who Is Carrie?*, and *The Clock*, all available in Yearling editions.

James Collier lives in New York City.
Christopher Collier lives in Orange, Connecticut.

P9-CAD-402

by
James Lincoln Collier
and
Christopher Collier

Published by
Bantam Doubleday Dell Books for Young Readers
a division of
Bantam Doubleday Dell Publishing Group, Inc.
1540 Broadway
New York, New York 10036

Maps by Jackie Aher

The trademark Laurel-Leaf Library® is registered in the U.S. Patent and
Trademark Office.
The trademark Dell® is registered in the U.S. Patent and Trademark Office.

ISBN: 0-440-21983-3

RL: 5.8

Reprinted by arrangement with Delacorte Press

Printed in the United States of America

January 1997

10 9 8 7 6 5 4

OPM

For Ida and Bonnie

ABOUT THE USE OF THE WORD "NIGGER" IN THIS BOOK

Over the long history of black people in America, a number of terms have been used for them. Until fairly recently the most acceptable word was Negro. Then, in the 1950s and 1960s, blacks decided that they preferred to be called *black*, and the term supplanted Negro. Another change came in the 1970s and 1980s, when *Afro-American*, and then *African American*, came to be preferred by some. These terms, however, have not entirely replaced *black*, which continues to be widely used.

Regrettably, the most common term for blacks has been, for well over two hundred years, *nigger*, a corruption of the word Negro. Until recent decades most whites in the North and virtually all in the South regularly employed this term, although in the North at least they might avoid using it in front of black people. Indeed, many blacks also use the term routinely among themselves, usually, but not always, in a half-joking or ironic way.

It is therefore impossible to completely avoid the term in a book of this kind, if we are to be historically accurate; many of the kinds of people portrayed here would have used that term, and no other. We hope readers will understand that we do not approve of the word, but have used it in order to present an accurate picture of black-white relations during the Civil War period.

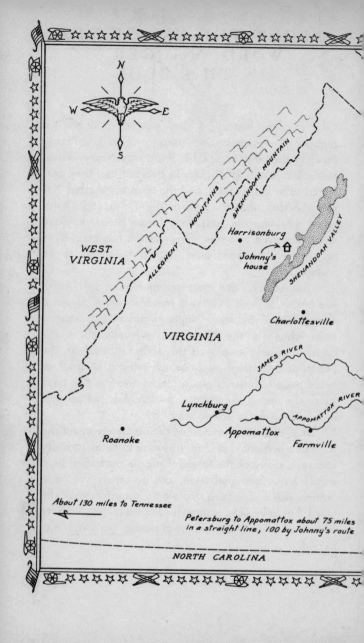

N
W   E
S

WEST
VIRGINIA

ALLEGHENY

MOUNTAINS

SHENANDOAH MOUNTAIN

Harrisonburg

Johnny's
house

SHENANDOAH VALLEY

VIRGINIA

Charlottesville

JAMES RIVER

Lynchburg

APPOMATTOX RIVER

Appomattox

Farmville

Roanoke

About 130 miles to Tennessee

Petersburg to Appomattox about 75 miles
in a straight line, 100 by Johnny's route

NORTH CAROLINA

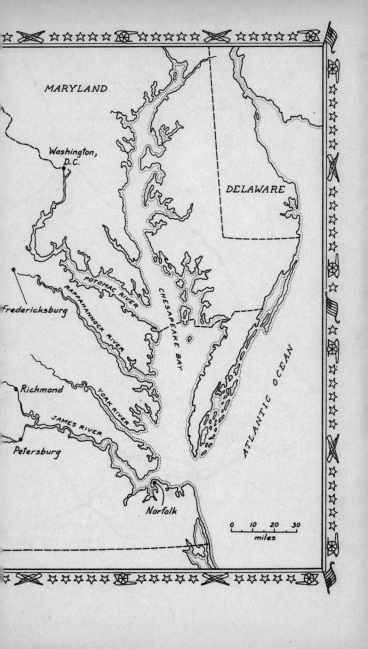

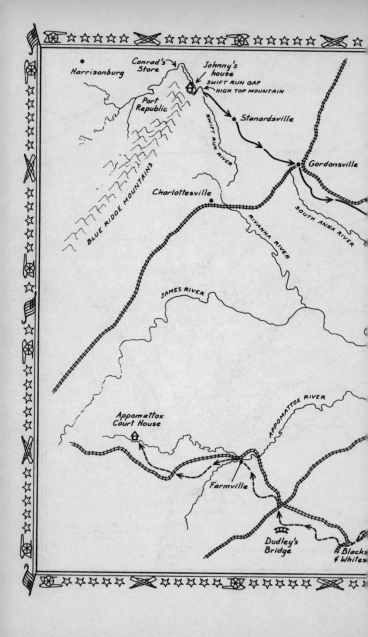

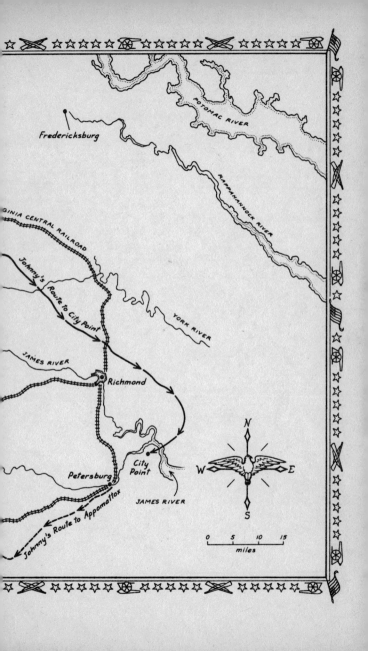

With Every Drop of Blood

Fondly do we hope, fervently do we pray,
that this mighty scourge of war may speedily pass away.
Yet, if God wills that it continue until all the wealth
piled by the bondsman's two hundred and fifty years
of unrequited toil shall be sunk, and until
every drop of blood
drawn with the lash shall be paid by another drawn
with the sword,
as was said three thousand years ago,
so still it must be said,
"The judgments of the Lord are true and righteous
altogether."

Abraham Lincoln
Second Inaugural Address
March 4, 1865

Chapter One

When they brought Pa home from the war all
shot up, he said he might die, and he did, too.
But before he did we had a lot of time to talk
about why he had to get himself shot—what
the war was about and why so many people
had to get killed in it. Hundreds of thousands
of them dead, Pa said. He wasn't exactly sure
how many, for it had been some time since
he'd read about it in the newspapers, but it
was way up there.

Pa got shot at a place called Cedar
Creek, which wasn't more than forty miles

from our house halfway up the side of High Top Mountain. If he had to get shot, it was good it happened nearby, for he didn't have far to travel to get home. He said it helped to stiffen his spine for the fighting to be near home, for he knew he was defending his own people—his own family, when you got down to it.

Oh, we needed defending, all right. The Shenandoah Valley was about as hard hit as any place during the war. The soil in the valley was rich and the crops always good—the barns busting out with corn, wheat, and hay, the cattle and hogs sleek and fat. The Southern army needed an awful lot of food every day and counted on the Shenandoah Valley to produce a good deal of it. Naturally, that brought on the Yankees. For months General Sheridan's bluecoats had been ranging up and down the valley, taking what they could carry off and destroying the rest—slaughtering our cattle and sheep, burning down our mills and whole barns full of corn and hay. It was awful. A crow would have to carry his own dinner if he was to fly across the Shenandoah Valley then.

We never thought they'd come up onto

our mountain, for our soil was thin and our crops not near as rich as down in the valley. One of the Reamer boys from down at Conrad's Store raced up to warn us that the Yankees were on their way. I hitched up the mules to the wagon. While I was harnessing them, Ma and the little ones, Sarah and Sam, threw everything they could lay their hands on into the wagon, and about five minutes later I was heading up High Top, across Hawksbill Creek, and into the woods above. And not a minute too soon, neither, for I wasn't more than a quarter mile into the woods when I heard the Yankee horses clattering over the stones on the wagon trail, and the sounds of somebody shouting orders. I fell down on my knees and prayed to the Lord they wouldn't think to look in the woods for me. They must have known, from seeing the hay and feed in our barn, that we had mules. But they didn't think of it, and by and by I heard them clatter on back down the wagon road. I waited another hour, just to be safe. Then I grabbed the lead mule, Bridget, by the halter and took them back down to the barn. We'd saved the mules, the wagon, and the stuff Ma and the little ones had thrown in the wagon—some tools, the plow, some bags of corn. But the Yankees had got our milch cow, which meant that nobody was going to get a cup of milk around there for a long time to come—not till the war was over, I reckoned.

Oh, I was mad as could be when I found out. What had we ever done to the Yankees to bring them down on us like that? I stood in the kitchen cussing them until Ma told me to stop it, I wasn't to take the Lord's name in vain no matter what the Yankees did. So I quit cussing, but I vowed that the next time I wasn't going to hide, but would fight them.

"With what?" Ma said, her lips tight.

"Great-grampa's sword," I said. Ma's grampa had fought in the Revolution. He'd been at the Battle of Yorktown, where the British surrendered, and got a sword from a British officer.

Ma gave a hard laugh. "One boy with a sword against a troop of bluecoats with repeating rifles."

"I'm not a boy. I'm fourteen."

"Johnny, you got to learn to rein yourself in. It says in Proverbs, 'He that is hasty of spirit exalteth folly.' You let your feelings run away with you too easy. You let go like that on a bunch of Yankees and you'll get yourself killed for it."

I knew Ma was right. So many had got killed in the war already one more didn't matter very much. The bluecoats wouldn't think twice about running me through with a bayonet if I started fussing with them. Still, it was hard to hold back your feelings while they rampaged around your place stealing things and smashing what they couldn't steal. All we could hope for was that General Early could push the Yankees out of the Shenandoah before we were stripped of everything. Of course, right then we didn't know that Pa was fighting along with General Early that very minute.

Up there on our mountainside life hadn't ever been easy. Pa'd always said that when Sam and Sarah got bigger and could do real farm work, he'd clear some more land and put in a cash crop. If we were lucky, we'd be able to put by a little money and buy a piece of land in the valley. But right now Sam and Sarah were too little to be much help, beyond taking care of the chickens and weeding the vegetable garden. With Pa gone, all the hard work fell on me and Ma. We plowed with the mules, planted, hoed, cut hay, and dug potatoes. The hogs weren't much of a bother most of the time, for we just turned them loose in the woodlot to feed off nuts and whatever else they could find. But still, you had to fatten them up in the fall, butcher them, salt the meat down, and cart what we didn't need for ourselves over to Stanardsville to sell.

Betweentimes I earned a little money with our mules and wagon, by hiring out as a teamster. I could handle those mules as well as a man. I was only ten when Pa left and didn't know much about it, but I'd seen him do it often enough, and had some idea of it. A lot of folks liked horses better than a mule team, but mules ate less and had more staying power than horses. And they were lighter and had smaller hooves, so they were much steadier on the mountains. I wouldn't have swapped 'em for anything. There were three of them—the lead mule was Bridget; then there was Regis, and Molly. They knew me and they'd do things for me they wouldn't do for anyone else. Oh, they could be stubborn, all right—stop dead on you the very time you were in a desperate hurry to get someplace. Bridget in particular had a mind of her own, and she'd stall for no reason I could see and wouldn't budge until I gave her a good talking to and cracked the whip at her in the bargain. When I did that, she'd turn and give me the most pitiful look you ever saw—why was she always getting blamed for everything? And if I was hungry and wanted to get home to supper, and wasn't in no mood for her shenanigans, I'd lose my temper and give her a good smack. I knew I should hold on to my feelings better, but sometimes I couldn't. I could manage the mules, but there's no easy way with them. Still, we were lucky to have them, and I took every teamstering job I could get, for we were short of money all the time. It was mighty hard doing without Pa.

He'd been fighting since the beginning. The moment the Virginia government voted to join with the other states that had seceded from the Union, he went out and signed up. He didn't think twice about it, for nobody figured the war would last more than a few months, and maybe not more than a few weeks. We could get along without him that long, he figured. But the war just went on and on. Pa was fighting at Manassas under General Stonewall Jackson, where we'd run the

Yankees clear back to Washington, nearly. After that he'd been at Gettysburg and climbed up a hill in an attack with the blue-coats firing down on him with everything they had. They almost drove the Yankees off that hill, Pa said, but the way the Yankees had got themselves dug in up there the Devil himself couldn't have driven them out. The bodies in the fields and orchards below were so thick you couldn't hardly put your foot down without tromping on one.

From time to time Pa managed to get home for a week or so. He'd rest up a bit, and then get to work on the farm straightening out things we hadn't been able to get to. Then he'd go, and we might not see him again for months. It went on like that for more'n three years.

Then, in the fall of 1864, there was terrible fighting up the valley to the north. We knew Pa was up there somewhere. Mr. Reamer came up to tell us about it. Sheridan had beat General Early good and the Yanks were all over the place down there now. But no word of Pa, and we were mighty worried. Then the wagon came up the trail, going in and out of the shadows made by the trees in the afternoon sun. At first we didn't think anything of it — there were always wagons going up and down by the house, for the best way east from that part of the Shenandoah was through Swift Run Gap up the mountain behind us. But of course Sam and Sarah were curious as usual. They ran down the wagon road to see who it was, and in a minute they were running back up to the house shouting, "It's Pa, it's Pa."

Well, we ran out, and sure enough it was him. He didn't look any too good. He was wrapped up in a blanket and hadn't shaved for some time, neither. His face was white and looked whiter because his black hair hadn't been cut for a while, and hung down by his cheeks.

The wagon stopped in front of our little stone house. Pa sat there looking at it, a smile on his face. "There were a lot of times I reckoned I'd never see the old place again."

Ma ran over to the wagon, put her arms around him, and hugged him. He winced. "Oof," he said.

Ma let him go. "You're hurt," she said.

"Pretty much so," he said. "I took a minié ball in my side. My luck ran out. I can't kick. I was lucky for three years. Some fellas didn't last three minutes." He looked at the house once more. "But now I'm back."

I liked our stone house, even if it was little—two rooms upstairs and two down, with the barn out back, the woodshed, root cellar, and all. The barn and the woodshed were made of planks, but the house was stone. On hot days it was cool and dark inside. I loved being inside there on days like that, when I got a chance, just sitting on Ma's footstool, listening to the clock tick, looking out the window where the sun poured down on the hayfield, hearing the bees buzzing in Ma's flower garden, feeling the cool and dark.

Even though it was warm for October and he was wrapped in a blanket, Pa shivered. "Johnny, help me down out of here." He nodded at the wagon driver. "And give this fella a cup of cider."

"There isn't any cider, Pa. The Yankees got it."

"The Yankees? They came up here?"

"Johnny took the mules and the wagon into the woods," Ma told him. "So we saved them. But they took the cow, the barrel of cider, a sack of corn we didn't get hid in time."

Pa shook his head. "I never thought they'd come up here." He swung his legs over the side of the wagon, wincing. "Give me your hand, Johnny. Let me down easy."

"Where does it hurt, Pa?"

He pointed to his left side, just below his ribs. "I got it right there."

I put my arm around him from the right side and eased him down out of the wagon. He stood there for a minute, holding on to the wagon to steady himself. "Thanks," he said to the driver. "I don't reckon I'd have made it up the mountain by myself."

"We owe you fellas that much," he said.

Pa let go of the wagon. The driver snapped his whip, and the horses began to tug the wagon on up the mountain past the house toward Swift Run Gap and the lowlands on the other side. Pa put his arm around my shoulder, and I helped him into the house. He eased himself into the old rocking chair by the stove in the kitchen. I wrestled up some wood to boost up the fire, and Ma fixed him some dinner. It wasn't much—boiled turnips and a piece of beef Ma'd managed to hide from the Yankees. "Don't worry," Pa said. "It beats hardtack and molasses. The Yankees pretty much cleaned out the valley—burned the mills and the barns full of wheat, stole the livestock. There's not much left for anybody down there now, us or them."

Then he told us how he got hit. "We were up the valley a ways, up past Massanutten Mountain. There's a little river up there they call Cedar Creek. The Yanks were camped to the north of it." He laid his knife on the table to stand for Cedar Creek. "We slipped across the creek before sunrise right here." He walked his fingers across the knife. "It was foggy and dark. They had no idea we were out there. We jumped on them and they broke and ran and we chased them out." He slid his fingers along the table top. "Finally we dug in at a place they call Belle Grove. But in the afternoon their cavalry came charging back at us." He galloped his fingers along the table. "We didn't have a chance. They rode right into us and we got up and ran back across Cedar Creek. It was an awful mess, our men trying to get through the creek with horsemen all around us, slashing with their sabers, and their infantry coming along behind, firing, and the wounded falling facedown in the creek and drowning." His fingers scrambled back and forth across the knife.

"Were you scairt, Pa?" Sam said.

"You bet I was. There wasn't never a man in battle who wasn't scared. Sometimes when the fighting's hot and you and them are right on top of each other shooting it out, you get so busy you forget to be scared. You don't forget when you're running for your life with the cavalry all around you slashing and shooting. All you can do is duck and dodge and pray to the good Lord to get you out in one piece. I ducked and dodged my way across the creek. I was just coming up the other bank when I felt the ball go into me." He stopped and looked out the window at the stubble in the hayfield, remembering. "It's funny," he said slowly. "All those years I saw men hit and a whole lot of them killed, too— hundreds of 'em, thousands, maybe—I don't know." He went on looking out the window, and I knew he was thinking about all those men who had died. "They call it 'seeing the elephant'—that means going into a fight. You march along strung out in a line, supposed to be thirteen inches apart, though I can tell you, once it gets hot you're not thinking about staying thirteen inches from the next man, or even worrying about where the next man is. You're thinking about those bluecoats up there behind a stone wall or over a creek and the balls flying all around you. Oh, you're scared, all right. But you wouldn't turn tail and run, for you've been with all those fellas around you for weeks and months, and you couldn't face them afterward if you did. So you keep on marching toward the guns, and here a man goes down and there another man goes down, but on you go until you're a couple of hundred yards from them. Then you begin to run and yell, and the men around you keep on falling, but you don't pay any attention, you just keep on running toward those guns up ahead, all the while loading and firing as best you can on the run. And either they give up and run on out of there, or it gets so hot you can't go any farther and you give up and crawl on back to where you started from."

We were all still as could be. Sarah and Sam stared at Pa, their mouths half open. I wondered if I'd be able to stand up to fighting like that. Pa went on looking out the window. "As many times as I see it happen, it took me by surprise. It was like getting slugged there with a club. I went numb, and the next thing I remember I was crawling up out of the creek holding on to myself where I'd got hit. My rifle was gone, I don't know where. I guess I dropped it in the creek when I got hit. It didn't matter, for I wasn't going to need it anymore. Then the numbness wore off and it began to hurt something awful. I crawled away and lay down behind some trees where I wasn't so likely to get run down by those Yankee horses. I sat there holding on to myself, biting into the collar of my shirt so as to keep from hollering out. But even so, every once in a while I'd hear this sound come out of me, like a cow bellering. It was funny—it didn't seem like I was making the noise—it was just coming out of me."

He stopped talking and looked at us.

"What happened next, Pa?" Sam said.

"I was lucky. The fighting passed on away and it wasn't more than an hour or so before the stretcher-bearers came along and carried me back to where they'd got a tent set up for the doctors. That wasn't much fun, being jolted along on that stretcher, but I got there by and by and they took the ball out of me and stitched me up. After that I lay in an old storehouse they'd fixed up for a hospital. In about a week I was well enough to bump along in a wagon without it hurting me too much. I picked up rides here and there to come home. Most people are glad enough to help a wounded soldier out. They'd share what they had." He looked at us all once more. "And here I be."

None of us said anything for a minute. Then I said, "How soon do you think you'll heal, Pa?"

He turned his head to look out at the sun shining down on the hayfield stubble. "That's up to the Lord, Johnny. 'What man is he that liveth and shall not see death?' Let's hope He sees fit to spare me."

Ma turned and walked out of the room. She didn't say anything, but I knew she was crying. That was when I began to wonder what the war was for.

Chapter Two

For a while it seemed like Pa was getting better. Ma tried to keep him fed as best she could, so as to give him strength to heal. After a couple of weeks he was getting around a little better, and even started to help with the chores some. He couldn't do any heavy work, like chopping wood or pitching hay, but he could do light work, like splitting kindling for the stove or currying the mules. Sometimes he helped Ma with the kitchen work. It was funny to see Pa doing women's work, like peeling potatoes. But he said Ma had done plenty of men's work while he was off fighting; turn about was fair play.

It was mighty hard to keep a farm going without a grown man around. Sarah and Sam did the best they could, but they were six and eight, and beyond the chickens, weeding, and maybe some berry picking in season, there wasn't much they could do. I'd learned a lot in the time Pa was gone—how to milk the cow and strip her teats clean of milk afterward so she wouldn't get infected, how to butcher a hog and get it ready for market, how to harness the mules and drive them. Mules take a lot of doing. They get used to one driver, and won't obey any other. Bridget, Regis, and Molly had got used to Pa, and I had to get them used to me. It took a while, but now I could get them to go anywhere—up a rocky slope, through the woods, down a steep trail. It was all in the way you talked to them.

Of course, it fell to me to cut all the wood for the house—chopping trees down in the woodlot, trimming off the branches, splitting the biggest logs with a maul and wedges, bringing the logs up to the house with the mules and wagon, and sawing them up on the sawbuck. Cold winter days I'd do that all day long, sunup to sundown, ten, twelve hours, until my legs ached and my arms were so tired I didn't think I could move them anymore. And the whole while a cold wind whistling through my clothes, freezing the sweat to my skin. Sometimes there'd be snow swirling around, too. By the middle of the afternoon I'd want nothing more in the world than to go home and sit by the fire, but knowing if I did, soon enough there wouldn't be any fire to sit by.

Our mistake was to think that the Yankees couldn't fight, and wouldn't fight if they could, and it'd all be over quick. At first everybody agreed with that. It was even in the newspapers: the Yankees hadn't the gumption for war. As soon as they saw the sun glittering off Southern bayonets, they'd turn tail and run. Everybody was certain of it. We'd be in Washington in a month, and the Federal government would hightail it up to Boston or someplace. Then our president Jeff Davis would sit down with old Abe Lincoln and tell him how *he* wanted things done. Everybody said it was bound to come out that way, for any good Southerner could whip a half dozen Yankees, easy.

But it didn't work out that way. Pa and I talked about it, sitting in front of the woodshed on the log pile while Pa showed me how to sharpen a saw. To tell the truth, I'd let the tools get pretty dull. Sharpening a saw or ax was fussy work and I wasn't very good at it. "Johnny, you're just making work for yourself using dull tools. See here? There isn't enough set to these teeth. You got to bend each one out just a little or the cut'll be too narrow and the wood'll bind the saw." He started to work on the teeth with a pair of pliers and I watched careful. "You got to learn these things, Johnny. Lots of hard times still ahead, that's for sure. Grant's got Bobby Lee penned up in Richmond, and he's closing the noose. Hard days to come."

I'd always figured we were bound to win in the end, but the way Pa was talking made me feel uneasy. "You don't think we could lose, Pa?"

"We still got a chance, I reckon. Bobby Lee's the greatest general there ever was. Everybody says that. If there's a way to win, he'll find it."

"But we fought so hard and lost so many men killed, it just isn't right for us to lose."

"Oh, we can lose all right. We were just plain dumb thinking the Yanks wouldn't fight, but would just roll over and die for us. They fought, all right. I saw them fight plain enough at Gettysburg. We should have had sense enough at the start to realize we couldn't beat them one to two, much less one to six, the way people around here were saying. If we could have beat them one to six, we'd have won years ago. But we couldn't. They're good fighters and there's a lot more of them than us."

He was making it sound worse and worse. "How much of a chance do you think we got, Pa?"

He shook his head slowly. "Can't tell, Johnny. Grant's having a shove at Petersburg, south of Richmond. Petersburg's the heart of Lee's supply lines into Richmond. If Petersburg goes, Richmond won't last a week. The only hope then'll be for Lee to give up Virginia, pull his army back down South, and see if he can hold out in the Carolinas and out west until the Yanks get tired of it."

"But then here in Virginia we'd be caught by the Yanks, Pa."

He nodded. "Could happen that way. It isn't just that they've got more troops than us. They've got a sight more factories than we have, and ships, and a navy. We never had anything you could really call a navy, not many of our own ships. We thought we were rich because we had cotton. Cotton was king, everybody said, the rest of the world couldn't get along without our cotton, and they'd do what we wanted so as to get it. Maybe the North didn't have cotton, but they had ships and factories for making rifles and cannon and shoes and railroad spikes."

"Even so, Pa, we almost had 'em beat once."

He nodded his head. "If we'd been able to bust through to Washington after Manassas right at the beginning, the way we almost did, we might have won. If we'd been able to get at them before they got their factories cranked up, we might have got them to settle with us—leave us alone to run things for ourselves. But we didn't, and they're plumb wearing us down. See this saw?" He shook it by the handle, making it rattle. "Even that's made up north—in Connecticut." He stared off toward the hayfield beyond the barn. "But we aren't giving up yet."

Now he held the saw up to his eyes and sighted along the teeth. "You got to make sure all the teeth are set the same, Johnny. Otherwise the widest one's be doing all the work for the rest. A sharp saw'll go through a log like a hot knife through butter, but one that ain't set right'll leave you with a sore arm for a week."

Suddenly it came to me that Pa was doing an awful lot of teaching me since he got back. Now that I thought of it, it seemed like he could hardly let a minute go by without giving me some advice on something. If we were just sitting on the back steps, resting a minute, he'd start in—the best way to straighten a bent nail, what kind of food to fatten hogs with, how to patch up a piece of harness that busted when you were on the road.

It wasn't just me, neither. At dinnertime he'd go to work on Sarah and Sam about their schooling. He'd make them read a couple of verses from the Bible, and then he'd take the book from them and have them spell out words to him. If it wasn't spelling, it was points of geography—what was the capital of France, and where Cuba was. Or arithmetic—two plus two for Sam, the times table for Sarah. The little ones would kick each other under the table and complained as much as they dared. But Pa said they'd missed half their schooling because of the war and had to catch up. He was specially strong on reading and writing. "Half the men I soldiered with couldn't write their own names if you put a gun to their head. Those fellas aren't going anywhere in life at all. They'll spend the rest of their born days behind a plow looking at the wrong end of a mule."

All this teaching scared me. It was like Pa figured he had only so much time to cram it all in, and had to keep at it every day. What would we do if Pa died? I hated to think about it. Of course, he was right, for if he died I'd be the man around the place and had to know how to do things. That was Pa: he always did things right and wouldn't give up on them till they *were* done right. I've seen the time when the plow hit a boulder in the field:

where another farmer would just plow around it and keep on going, Pa'd wrestle that ornery thing out of there. Ma always said, "Your Pa hates to leave a thing until he's got it right." What would we do if he died? And then suppose we lost the war anyway—he'd have died for nothing.

I couldn't ask him about that straight out, so instead I said, "Pa, are you sorry you joined up?"

He looked out past the barn to the hayfield again, squinting. "Johnny, that's a hard one. I thought about it a good deal. Of course, a man's got a duty to fight for the honor of his country. I couldn't let the other men go and sit home safe myself while they did the fighting for me. I got too much respect for myself to do that. The Bible says, 'A time to love, and a time to hate; a time of war, and a time of peace.' Sometimes you can't get around things. But a man's got other things to look after along with the honor of his country—his wife and kids, his neighbors, his church. When it started, there wasn't a question in my mind but I had to join up. Your ma didn't want me to go, but she saw that I had to. But if I'd a known at the start how long it would go on and how bad it would be, I might a thought twice. I hate to see you all working so hard and growing up without me around to see that you get raised proper."

"If only those Yankees weren't so blame hot to turn the darkies loose."

"Believe me, Johnny, I didn't go out there and get myself shot over a passel of nigras. That wasn't the point of fighting. Why would I fight for slavery? We don't have slaves, nor do half the people in the valley, neither. And most of them who do, don't have more than one or two and could get along just as well without them. Better, more'n likely. Half your slaves aren't worth the trouble. You got to feed 'em and clothe 'em and doctor 'em when they're sick and can't work. And you got to watch over 'em every minute to get any work out of 'em. I wouldn't have a slave on this place if you gave him to me."

"The newspapers always say that slavery's part of the Southern way of life and we can't give it up."

"You don't want to believe everything you read in the papers, Johnny. Oh, I reckon them mighty fellas with their big houses and thousand-acre spreads figure they need their slaves. But blame me if I can see the sense of it. Pay a white man a fair wage, and he'll give you twice as much work as any nigra, and you don't have to feed and clothe him, in the bargain."

"Then what's the war for, Pa?"

"Why, you wouldn't want us to just roll over and die in front of the Yankees, would you, Johnny? The U.S. Constitution says each state is equal, and if Virginians let the Federals take away our slaves or say we can't take them into the new territories out west, there's no telling where they'll stop. Next thing you know the Federal government will try to tell us what to grow or who we can sell our cotton and tobacco to. No, Johnny, this here war isn't about slaves at all—it's about a state's right to govern itself."

Well, that made sense. Why should the Federal government tell us what to do? "I wouldn't want them bossing me around," I said.

"Well, there it is. The way it used to be, things were even between the North and the South. But things have changed. Now the North has the most states and the most people and has got rich from all those factories and such. They can outvote us in Congress whenever they want. If you give 'em the chance, they'll run the whole country to suit themselves — North, South, Injun territories, and everything else. That isn't the way George Washington and Jimmy Madison and those other fellas set it up. I know what Jimmy Madison would have said if he could see the way the North has got the upper hand and was trying to push us around. He'd say it wasn't right. He'd say the states weren't beholden to the Federal government, that they're free and independent. That's what the war is all about — states' rights, the way it says in the Constitution. Why, Jimmy Madison got a whole amendment added to the Constitution just to make sure the states hung on to their rights."

"What's that, Pa?"

He shook his head. "The tenth amendment is what it was. I can't quote it right off exact. But the meaning of it is, the Federal government can't interfere whenever it wants in a state's own business."

"Like what?"

"Well, like — if we can or can't have

slaves," Pa said. "That's for each state to decide."

I was getting sort of confused. "You said the war isn't about slavery."

"It isn't," Pa said. "You got to see the difference, Johnny. It isn't about whether we can keep slaves. It's about who decides—the states or the Federals. My pa told me that when I was just a tad, and he was right." He put his hand on my shoulder and looked me straight in the face. "Johnny, life won't be nothing for us if the Yanks take over down here. We'd be worse off than the nigras, for they don't know what it's like to be your own man. But a white person, who's lived free and independent, he won't be able to stand it."

"Pa, why are the Yankees so dreadful set on coming down here and pushing us around?"

He spit. "Some of 'em are all fired up about slavery. But a lot of them very Yanks that are down here getting themselves shot to pieces don't want nigras around any more than I do. You ought to hear them talk."

"Did you ever talk to any Yanks, Pa?"

"Sure I did, Johnny. You got to remember, we won a few fights ourselves. We captured a good many of 'em, and even picked up their wounded. Some of 'em are hot to end slavery, but a lot of 'em, so far as I could judge, don't much care about it one way or another."

"Then what are they in it for?"

"I don't rightly know, Johnny. Course the rich fellas that own the factories want to get hold of our cotton cheap, so they probably like the idea of slavery. But you take an ordinary mill hand, some of 'em were saying that it kept their wages down when the South had unpaid workers, but I don't know if that's right. Maybe it's the pioneers who don't want slavery out on the Plains."

"Why didn't the Yanks try it before?"

"They couldn't, before, Johnny. We equaled them in strength. But as soon as they got the edge on us, they wanted to take over." He looked off down to the hayfield once more. "Whatever else there is to it, a man who took any pride in his Southern honor couldn't sit still for it, no matter what the odds were."

At least that was something I could understand.

Chapter Three

Pa lingered on through the fall. Sometimes he seemed a little better and would go out to the woodshed and try to split some wood, or curry the mules. If he could help at all, he would. Other times he'd take for the worse. It'd hurt him so much to walk around he'd stay in bed. He always got up for meals, no matter how bad he felt. He wasn't a baby, he said, to be fed in bed—he'd get up and eat like a man. But he wouldn't eat much—not that there was a whole lot to eat anyway— and go right back to bed.

For years all of us had got down on our knees every morning before breakfast and every night before bed—Sarah, Sam, Ma and me—and prayed to the Lord to bring him home to us. Now he was home and nothing was changed. Ma and me were still stuck with all the work, and more of it than ever, for there was Pa to take care of now—wash him when he felt too poorly to wash himself, help him get dressed in the morning when he felt good enough to get up.

I got a fair amount of teamster work that fall, for the bluecoats had taken a lot of people's horses and mules. The ones that still had stuff to sell—corn or apples or cider or something—had to get it over to Stanardsville or Port Republic. They needed me. In peacetime those farmers down in the valley were mighty prosperous and would haul off to market wagonload after wagonload of corn and hay and cured pork or beef. But now, of course, the Yanks had stolen their horses and wagons, like as not. It was sorrowful to see them loading onto my wagon nothing but a couple of baskets of dried apples or a few thin slices of beef, so that the wagon wasn't half filled. And it wasn't a big wagon, neither—three feet wide and six feet long, covered over with a canvas tent four feet high. But it meant a little money for us, and I was mighty glad to have the work.

One time I was gone for three nights hauling a wagonload of corn from over at Harrisonburg through Port Republic and Brown's Gap and on down to Charlottesville. I didn't get back until after dark of the fourth day. Ma heard the wagon swing around back to the barn and came out. I got down from the wagon. She put her hand on my arm. "Pa's took real bad," she said. "You better go see him."

"I will," I said. "Soon as I get the mules unhitched and fed."

"No. Go now. I'll see to the mules."

I felt myself grow scared and cold. "How bad is Pa?"

"He's bad. You better go quick. He wants to tell you something."

My heart beating fast, I went in. Pa was lying in bed, propped up with a couple of pillows. His breath was coming fast, his face was white and wet with sweat. The candle by the bed flickered as I came in, and a ray of light crossed his face. Back in the shadows in a corner Sarah and Sam sat squeezed in side by side in the old rocking chair, not saying anything, just watching.

"Johnny?" Pa said. His voice was soft and hoarse.

"Yes, Pa."

"I can't see too good anymore," he said in that hoarse voice. "Hold the candle up."

I picked it up off the little table by the bed and held it up. The room brightened a bit, and I could see the little ones better. They were scared, their faces white, and there were smudges of tears on their cheeks. I looked at Pa. "That's better," he said.

"Can you see me, Pa?"

"More or less. Good enough. I can see where you are, anyway."

"I'm sorry I was gone so long," I said. "I had to go all the way down to Charlottesville. It took longer than I reckoned on."

"It's all right," he said. What with his breath coming so fast it wasn't easy for him to talk. "I'm glad you got back in time. I was scared you wouldn't."

"Maybe you'll get better, Pa. Maybe it'll pass."

"No. Not this time. I'll be gone soon."

He coughed. "Johnny, over the past while I did a lot of talking about states' rights and the honor of the South and such. I wish I hadn't." He coughed again.

"Why, Pa?"

"It's bound to get you riled up to fight."

"Pa, anybody'd get riled up to fight after what the Yankees did around here. It wasn't just what you said. 'An eye for an eye and a tooth for a tooth,' it says in the Bible."

"Even so, I wish I hadn't." He reached out his hand and I took it. It felt cold and damp. "Johnny, I want you to promise me something."

If I hated the Yankees before, I hated them worse now. "I'll get even with them for you, Pa."

He coughed again, and shook his head. A kind of shudder went over him. "Water," he whispered.

"Sam, get Pa some water."

Sam darted away.

"I knew that's what you were thinking, Johnny," Pa said. "I knew you were bound to let your feelings run away with you, and might go off to fight. You got to promise me you won't. I took care of our duty to Virginia.

I took care of the honor of the South. You got to see to our duty to the family. Ma can't take care of the little ones alone. You got to help." He began to cough again.

"Pa—"

He held up his hand until he was done coughing, and I stayed still. Then he whispered, "You got to promise me, Johnny."

Sam came in with a dipper full of water. I took it from him and held it up to Pa's mouth. He took a few sips, but he was having trouble swallowing and couldn't drink much. "Pa, let me sit you up a little higher, so's you can drink."

He shook his head and pushed the dipper away. "It doesn't matter. I can stand a dry throat a little bit longer." He looked at me for a minute. "Now, Johnny, promise."

There wasn't anything else I could do. "I promise, Pa."

"You promise you won't get any foolish notions about running off to fight for the honor of the South."

"I promise."

"And you'll stay to home and see to things here." He coughed again. "The little ones."

"I promise." I hated to, for there wasn't anything I wanted more right then than to run a sword through a couple of Yankees.

He took my hand again and squeezed it. "I trust you, Johnny." He shivered and coughed. I waited till he was done. "All right, go help your ma with the mules. I guess I'll last a little longer."

I hurried outside. Ma had got the mules out of harness and into the stalls. She was up in the haymow pitching down some hay for them.

"I'll do that, Ma. You go on in and tend to Pa."

She put the pitchfork down and clambered down the haymow ladder. "What did he want to tell you?"

"He made me promise not to run off to fight. He made me promise to stay here and help with things."

"I figured that was it," she said. "Did you promise?"

"Yes."

"I'm glad," she said. She put her arms on my shoulders and looked me square in the face, for we were about the same height. "It'd kill me to lose another one, Johnny."

Then we heard a shriek from inside the house. The kitchen door slammed open and Sarah busted into the barnyard. "Ma, Ma," she screamed. "Pa's dead."

Mr. Reamer over at Conrad's Store made the coffin for us, just a plain pine coffin. I said I'd do some teamstering for him to pay for it. I picked it up. We put Pa in and I nailed the top on. Then we drove over to the little Baptist church in Port Republic where we went. To be honest, we didn't get over there very often, for it was ten miles over and ten miles back. We didn't have any money for a stone, so I made a cross of wood and lettered on it Pa's name and his dates—1825–1864. It wasn't very pretty, for I wasn't much of a hand at sign painting, but I figured when the war was over and I was grown and had some money, I'd buy him a regular headstone.

Riding home from the cemetery was the hardest thing I ever did in my life. It felt like I was tied back there to that wooden cross by a string from my guts. Ma had got over crying and the little ones sat quiet—I don't think they really understood it. But my feelings busted loose. I couldn't stop crying and cried for near an hour before I could get hold of myself. Pa meant that much to me.

It was a long time before I felt better, too. Oh, how I wanted to get at those Yankees for it. I thought about it all the time, catching one of 'em alone and chopping at him with Great-grampa's sword.

But the weeks went along. Christmas came and went, and bit by bit I stopped thinking about Pa all the time, and what the worth of it was. The truth was, I didn't have much time to think about anything, for it was about all we could do that winter to scrape together dinner every day and get up enough firewood to keep the house warm. The Federal troops under Sheridan had driven General Early out of the Shenandoah and stripped it. They wanted food for their own troops, of course, but the main idea was to starve the South out so we'd have to quit fighting. A lot of darkies went with them, too. They said that since Lincoln had freed the slaves, slavery was illegal and they were contraband. But folks generally agreed that was just a fancy word for taking people's property, no different from taking their horses and hay.

We just managed. We had enough potatoes to last for a while and some beef that Ma had hid from the Yankees that time. In the early spring I sent Sam and Sarah out to collect fiddlehead ferns, enough for two or three meals, and later there were dandelion greens, too. But that was all the vegetables we'd have until we got the garden in.

The one thing good about the shortages was that if you had anything to spare, you could get an awful big price for it. Things of every kind were scarce—shoes, corn, cloth, thread, nails. Anything you want to name, there was a shortage of it. Salt was going for sixty dollars a sack, where before the war it was a dollar and a half. Oh, the Yankees had messed us up good; I'd have given anything to have a crack at them. Sometimes I even wished they'd come back up on our mountain and jump me, for then I'd have to fight them, no matter what I promised Pa.

Then, along about the middle of March, when things were beginning to warm up a little, I went over to Stanardsville with a couple of barrels of cider for somebody. Stanardsville was down the other side of the mountain from the Shenandoah Valley, and hadn't been as hard hit. There was still a mill standing there, a couple of stores, and most of the town still going. I delivered my cider to one of the stores, and after I finished unloading it, I sat down on the porch, with my legs dangling over, to rest a little before I started for home again. Just then out of the store came a teamster I'd seen there before. "Hello, youngster," he said.

"Hello, Jeb."

"How's things back home?"

"We're managing, but it's awful close," I said. "How about you?"

"So long as there's teamstering work, I'll get along. Provided them Yankees don't come along and shoot me off my wagon."

"They mostly don't shoot people. Starve 'em to death, maybe, but they don't shoot 'em."

"Depends," Jeb said. "We're plannin' on gettin' up a wagon train to bring food into Richmond. I don't doubt but that the Yankees'll shoot first and ask questions later if they ketch up with that one."

That perked me up some. Richmond was where President Jeff Davis and the Confederate government was. A lot of folks figured it would be safer to have our capital way down south in Atlanta or someplace, but old Jeff Davis was determined to show the North he wasn't afraid of them, so he put the capital in Richmond, which wasn't more than sixty or seventy miles from the Yankee border— maybe a hundred miles from Washington itself. Naturally, the Yankees were hot to capture our capital, but they hadn't done it yet— General Lee was too much for them. "What's the plan of it, Jeb?"

"They reckon to set out from here in a week or so—soon as they round up enough wagons."

"You going?"

"I reckon. Pay'll be mighty good 'cause there's a risk to it. I guess I'll chance it. Anyway, I got a duty to do it. So long as I'm willing to teamster, I don't have to put on a uniform."

"What if you come across Yankees?"

"They're going to send some of Mosby's Rangers along as guards. They ought to be able to fend off the Yankees."

Mosby's Rangers were famous. Colonel Mosby and his bunch were fighting pretty much on their own around Virginia. They lived off the land. They'd race into a bluecoat camp, shoot the place up, grab whatever they could find loose, and race away before the bluecoats knew what hit them. Or they'd follow along behind a Union army, picking off stragglers and shooting up the supply wagons coming along behind. They were dreadful fearsome, and the Yankees were afraid of them. "I don't see what the risk would be if you have the Mosbys along."

"That's what I reckon, but you never can tell. There's bound to be some risk."

"How do they figure on getting into Richmond if it's surrounded?"

"There's still holes where you can get in and out. That's where the real risk comes in, for once we get close, there'll be Yanks everywhere." He squinted at me. "You thinking about coming along, youngster?"

Well, I was. The idea of it excited me. It was a chance to get even with the Yankees for what they did to Pa. Besides, I hated the idea that Jeb and a lot of other fellas were in on things, and I was kept out of them. But there wasn't any way around it. "I promised Pa when he lay dying that I wouldn't fight, but would stay home and look after the little ones."

"We ain't aimin' to fight," Jeb said. "It's just teamstering."

That was so. I was getting tempted. Still, it might come to fighting. "I don't know."

"Mighty good pay for a few days' work, it looks like."

That was another point. "We sure could use the money."

"Whyn't you go talk to the major?" He pointed over his shoulder to the door to the store. "He's just in there."

Well, I knew I shouldn't go. It was teamstering, not fighting, that was true. Still, there was a chance of getting shot or captured or something, and where'd Ma and the little ones be then? But blame me if I didn't want to go in the worst way.

But I shouldn't. I stood up, resolved to get out of there before I gave in to myself. And just then there came out of the store a white-haired man with a short white beard. He limped a little and walked with a cane. Jeb stood up and took off his hat. "Hello, Major."

"Hello, Jeb. You going to be in the party for Richmond?" He had a loud, crackling voice.

"Reckon so, Major." He pointed to me with his thumb. "Here's another one you might recruit."

He turned and gazed at me. I stood up, too. "You have a team and a wagon, son?"

"Yes, sir," I said, pointing. "Those are my mules."

"Good. We need every wagon we can get."

"Sir, I promised my pa when he was dying I'd stay home and take care of Ma and the little ones."

"Your pa? What did he die of?" he said in that loud voice.

"He was wounded at Cedar Creek, and died of it after he came home."

In my heart I was hoping the Major'd come up with some reason why I had to go. I wondered if dead people really looked down on you the way some people said. I hoped Pa wasn't looking down on me right then.

"Surely he'd want you to help against the Yankees."

"He said he'd done our share of the fighting, it was up to me to take care of the family, since he wouldn't be there to do it."

"A lot of people have suffered and died. Your ma will have to endure it if it comes to that. You have a duty to Virginia. That comes first over everything. No Southerner can neglect his duty and keep his honor."

I wondered what Pa would say to that. I knew of families in the valley where they'd lost two or three men, and the women and children had to get along as best they could. "I don't know, sir. I promised him when he was dying. I'd hate to go back on a promise like that."

He banged his cane on the porch floor. "He shouldn't have made you promise that. It's your duty to Virginia that's in question. You can't make a promise against that."

I could hear Pa, just as clear as if he was there, saying that he'd taken care of our duty to Virginia. But I wanted to go in the worst way. "I'll ask Ma. Maybe she'd let me go if there wasn't too much of a risk in it." I was hoping the major'd say it was safe as churches.

But he didn't. "A man of honor doesn't

ask what the risk is, he asks where his duty lies."

Suddenly Jeb put in, "Tell your ma it's four hundred dollars—that ought to carry some weight with her."

If I convinced Ma that there wasn't any risk to it, but a good deal of money, she might agree. "How many Mosbys are going along?"

"I heard it was fifty," Jeb said.

That seemed like a good number. "I'll talk to Ma," I said.

I thought about it hard all the way home. Would the Yankees dare attack us if we were guarded by fifty Mosbys? Besides, the Yankees didn't know the countryside and the Mosbys did, and could guide the wagon train along little back roads the Yanks wouldn't know about. And when you figured the amount of money I could bring home, it was hard to see how I couldn't go. After all, what better could I do for the family than earn all that money, especially as there wasn't much risk in it? Suppose the bluecoats came up on our mountain again and cleaned us out altogether. The little ones would go hungry, and maybe starve, unless we had some money tucked away where the bluecoats couldn't find it. When you looked at it that way, it seemed like it was my *duty* to the family to go to Richmond. Pa was certain to see that.

It was a pretty good argument. But deep down, I felt kind of uneasy. How risky really was it? Would Pa really agree that I had a duty to go? Was he looking down on me? God looked down on you, I knew that. God knew everything that was going on everywhere. To be honest, I didn't see how He could do it—keep that many people straight in His head, saying nothing of the cats, dogs, leaves, stones, rivers, and I don't know what all else. But the Bible said He could, and so did the preacher, and I figured they knew a blame sight more about it than I did.

So I knew God was listening to me thrash it out with myself. But was Pa? Or was he just dead? I took a quick look upward, half afraid I'd see Pa's face up there staring down at me. There was nothing but a cloudy sky. Still, I blushed when I did it, and looked back down at the mules again.

When I got home I gave Ma all the arguments—how it was safe as churches, and could make a lot of money.

She set her lips and shook her head.

"Don't even think about it, Johnny. You promised your pa."

"But it isn't the same as fighting, Ma. I'm not going to fight, just drive the mules. Pa'd want me to do it, so as to get money for the family. Suppose the bluecoats come back and clean us out? It's for the little ones. Pa would say so himself." Well, Pa wouldn't have said that. But the feeling to go was on me so strong I couldn't help what I was saying.

"How much could you earn?"

"Four hundred dollars, Jeb says."

Her eyes widened. "That much? Which Jeb is that?"

"Wagner. From over to Stanardsville."

"He's going?" she said. "I don't know him well, but he seems like a sensible man."

"He says there'll be fifty Mosbys to guard us. It'll be safe as churches." I began to blush again, for Jeb didn't say that. He said there was a risk in it. But Ma'd never let me go if I said so.

She nodded. "I'll speak to Isaac Reamer to see if he thinks it's safe."

"It's my duty to Virginia," I said. I blushed again when I said it.

She gave me a look. "There's no rush.

How many times have I told you, 'He that is hasty of spirit exalteth folly.' I'll ask Isaac Reamer when I have a chance."

A couple of days later we went over to Conrad's Store to see Mr. Reamer. He had a little cider left and we had a cup of it sitting in a patch of sun on his back steps. "You say Jeb Wagner's going, Johnny?"

"Yes. He was the one who gave me the idea."

"And he thinks it'll be safe?"

"He says we'll have fifty Mosbys with us." That was true.

"The Mosbys ain't magic," he said. "You sure Jeb thinks there's no danger?"

"I reckon he wouldn't be going if he figured it was risky." I took out my pocket hanky and dabbed at my eye, like I had something in it, so they couldn't see my face.

Ma said, "How long would it take Johnny to get over there and back?"

"Four, five days each way, I reckon. You can't be sure, for they'll probably have to go along back roads and such."

She thought. "I could spare him that

long, I guess. But not much longer." She looked at me. "You're sure about the Mosbys?"

"That's what Jeb said." I hoped that Pa wasn't looking down at me just then.

Chapter Four

I left a week later with the mules and the wagon. I'd put a little time into seeing that the wagon was in good shape. One of the wooden hoops that held up the canvas had split, and I took it out and bound up the split. I patched a couple of holes in the canvas, and greased the axles, for if you didn't grease them regular every day they made an all-fired awful screeching as the wheels went around. And I fed the mules up good, for all they'd get to eat along the way was whatever grass they could snatch at. I even gave Bridget a couple of last year's old, dried apples to put her in a good temper. She loved apples, and if I happened to be eating one when I was currying them or harnessing them up, she'd put her nose right up to my face to see if she could get a bite. Generally I'd end up giving her the core anyway.

The wagon road went through the Blue Ridge Mountains by way of Swift Run Gap, up and down hills on the narrow dirt road. It was rough countryside, mostly woods, with here and there a lonely farmhouse and barn sitting in the midst of fields and orchards, where somebody had carved a farm out of the woods. But it was pretty all the same, hawks floating in the sky high up, little streams purling through the woods and over the road to run on down the mountainside. I'd driven the mules through it lots of times, and I always liked to see it.

But this time it was different. I wasn't just going to Stanardsville with a load of corn, I was doing something for the honor of Virginia and the whole South against the Yankees. I looked back into the empty wagon. Great-grampa's sword was stuck through a loop of rope I'd rigged up, where I could grab it fast if I had to. Ma didn't know it was there.

She thought it was still stuck down in the hay in the hayloft where we hid it from the bluecoats. I wished I dared wear it in my belt, but I didn't, for if I twisted the wrong way I might stick Regis, the mule I was riding on.

Besides the sword, I'd stuck a little book of psalms in my pocket, so's I had something to while away the time with, for it was going to be a lot of long days with nothing much to do but sit on Regis and look around.

I knew I ought to feel sinful for what I'd done—telling Ma that Jeb said there wasn't any risk to it. But I didn't. I felt brave and daring, like one of King Arthur's knights off on an adventure. It was the first time I'd felt happy since Pa died, and after a while I started to sing at the top of my lungs:

> In Dixieland where I was born in,
> Early on one frosty mornin',
> Look away, look away,
> Look away, Dixieland . . .

But I couldn't do much singing, for the mules liked for me to pay them some attention. Bridget was out front to lead, with Regis and Molly side by side just in front of the wagon. I generally rode on Regis, although at times I'd get off and walk, especially when they were pulling uphill or over a bad piece of road and the going was slow. Mules aren't really ornery, the way a lot of folks think. It's just that they have their own ideas about things. They're real smart, too. Once you get to know them, you understand their likes and dislikes, and you can generally persuade them to go along with you.

For example, Bridget was a real tourist and liked to take in the sights. Every so often she'd stop to look around. I'd learned it was best to give her a minute or two to look at the view. Then I'd give her a special shout I had for her—sort of "ayeeeooo." It was a kind of warning that she'd had her look and would get a lick behind her ears with the whip if she didn't start moving. Mules are mighty testy about those long ears. They don't like it any to have people fussing with them.

With one thing and another it was near nightfall by the time I reached Stanardsville. I went around to the store, where they loaded the wagon with beef packed in wooden barrels. Then they told me to head off through town until I came out the other side, where

I'd see some teamsters camped in a woods. I was to wait there until the wagon train formed up over the next day or so.

It was dark when I got there. There were a few campfires spotted around the woods, with two or three teamsters at each one. I pulled into the woods, unhitched the mules, and curried them with the brush I brought along—you got to curry the mules regular, or their pores'll clog up with dirt and sweat. By the time I got finished I was good and tired; it had been a hard day. I ate a chunk of bread and cheese I brought along, had a pull from my water jug, rolled up in my blanket, and went to sleep in the wagon.

When I got up in the morning I saw that three or four more wagons and teams of horses had come in during the night. There was nothing much for me to do but wait.

Along about noon Jeb Wagner rolled into the woods with his wagon. I gave him a chance to get his horses settled, and then I walked over to where he was hunkered down on his haunches with two other teamsters, chewing the fat. They were arguing about a wagon train they'd been in—when it had been and where it had been, and who had been in it.

"No, Jeb," one of them said. "You ain't got a brain in your head. It wasn't nowhere near to Port Royal, it was just west of Winchester. I remember it, because when we was riding through town I seen a sign *Winchester Soap Company*, and I thought to myself, 'Why that was Granny's name.'"

"What was, Baldy?" Jeb said. "Soap?"

"No, you idjit, Winchester. That was Granny's name."

The third one put in, "I'll be blamed if I knew you could read, Baldy."

"Sure, Baldy can read," Jeb said. "And write, too. I seen him practicing writing his own name. Got it right a couple of times, too." He gave me a glance to see if I appreciated his joke and I smiled, so as to let him know I did.

"How come you knew he got it right, Jeb?" the third one said. "You was having trouble figuring out which day of the week it was the last time I seen you. I believe you don't know the days of the week."

"Oh, yes, he does too," Baldy said. "I

heard him saying them over to hisself the other day. He knows every last one o' 'em. Now all he's got to do is put 'em in the right order."

The third one nodded. "He'll do it, too. Just give him time. Then he can start on the months. That's a sight harder, for there's only seven days, but heaps of months to keep in line. I doubt if you'll be able to manage, Jeb."

"All right," Jeb said, "if you're so wicked smart, let's hear which months has thirty days and which ones has thirty-one."

"Oh I know that. It's easy. Lemme ask you how many days February has."

Jeb thought about it a minute. "Thirty," he said.

Before I could stop myself I blurted out, "Twenty-eight, except on leap year when it has twenty-nine." Before I even finished saying it I wished I'd kept my mouth shut.

Jeb looked kind of sour, but Baldy began to laugh. "You two fellas think you're so powerful smart and here comes some bitty fella that's hardly out of his crib, knows more than you do."

I didn't much like being called a bitty

fella, but I'd brought it on myself. "I'm fourteen," I said.

Baldy squinted at me. "Ain't you a little young to be getting yourself mixed up in a jaunt like this?"

"My Pa was killed by the Yanks and I aim to get even for him."

Baldy looked me up and down. "I don't doubt but what you got the fighting spirit in you, but what're you going to fight the Yanks with—your teeth?"

"I got my great-grandpa's sword. He got it in the Revolution."

The three of them busted out laughing. I went red. "What's wrong with a sword? All the officers have them."

"That's for jabbing at their own troops when they break and run. Them swords was all right for King Arthur, but they ain't much use against a repeater rifle. Old Billy Yank'll have six holes in you before you get close enough to throw it at him, much less stick him with it."

I felt pretty foolish and resolved I wouldn't mention Great-grampa's sword again. "Well, anyway, I'm going to fight them if I get the chance."

"Bound to get revenge for your pa, is it?" Jeb said.

I wondered. Was that the whole reason? Everybody seemed to have a different idea of it—states' rights, honor of the South, slavery. Why were these fellas in it? Of course, they weren't soldiers, but so long as they were carrying goods for our side, they were taking a risk. "Pa said we got to fight for states' rights."

"Well, I don't know about states' rights," Jeb said. "That's all too much for me. What I won't stand for is having a nigger put up as good as a white man. I don't care what old Abe says, there never lived a nigger that was as good as a white man. If them Yankees want them black bucks sittin' down to dinner with them, why, that's their business. But they ain't gonna tell me I have to do it. You can't trust a nigger far as you can throw him."

Baldy looked solemn and nodded. "That's God's truth, Jeb. If He'd of wanted them to sit down with the white man, He wouldn't of made them black. He done it so as they could be told apart from whites. It's right there in the Bible. Noah put a curse on

Canaan and turned him black, and that's where niggers come from."

"Baldy, you don't know no more about it than you do the days of the months. It wasn't Canaan, it was Cain, and it wasn't Noah who cursed him and turned him black, it was God. Cain, he walloped his brother and the Lord turned him black for it."

It was plain to me that neither of them knew the first thing about it. We didn't get to church all that much, because of it being so far away, but all those years I was growing up, Pa read a chapter out of the Bible every morning before breakfast and every night before bed. After Pa went to fight, Ma did it, too. I reckoned we'd got through the whole thing three or four times, though I wasn't sure. I knew the story of Cain and Abel and the story of Noah and Canaan, too, and I couldn't see where it had anything to do with the colored.

But it didn't seem sensible to start explaining the Bible to these fellas, so I said, "Over where I come from most folks don't have any slaves. It doesn't much matter to them whether the colored are free or not. Letting Virginia have her constitutional rights is what they care about."

Baldy looked me up and down. "They'll get over that the first time some big buck comes walking down the sidewalk pushing white folks into the street. Yessir, I'm for states' rights, all right—states' rights to keep their slaves."

Jeb yawned. "Blame me if I couldn't use a little drink just now. Where's that whiskey jar of yours, Baldy?"

It seemed like a good time to leave and I skedaddled. It was confusing, all right. How come some people were fighting for one reason and some for another? To be honest, I wasn't so sure all those people back home were as hot for states' rights and the Constitution as Pa was. I never heard much talk about it. It seemed like a lot of people were fighting the Yanks just because they were here.

Chapter Five

The Mosbys clattered into the woods on horseback toward suppertime. They were pretty fierce looking, all right. They were dressed every which way—some of them wearing regular Confederate uniforms, or at least parts of uniforms, some of them in ordinary shirts and trousers, some of them wearing pieces of clothing they'd captured from the Federal bluecoats. A lot of them had beards and moustaches, and most of them had big Bowie knives tucked into their belts, along with a pair of Colt .44 revolvers. Some of them had another pair of Colts stuck into the tops of their boots. I could see why they scared the Yankees, for they scared me, and I was on their side.

We spent two days in that patch of woods, waiting for more wagons filled with supplies to come in. We were all a little nervous just resting there, for we'd be sitting ducks for Federal troops. But the Mosbys kept scouts out circling around and about.

On the third day we got up while it was still dark and got ready to move out. That early in the morning nobody was doing much talking. We got little fires going and boiled up coffee. Those who had a little beef or bacon fried it up. Those who didn't had to content themselves with hardtack.

I harnessed up the mules. It's not easy if you aren't used to it, but I could do it with my eyes closed. First you slip the collar over the mule's head. Then you slide the harness on, fasten up the lines, and hitch the evener to the shaft. You got to make sure that everything's not too tight, not too loose. You get a knack for it after a while.

Then, as the sky began to lighten up, we moved out. Some of the Mosbys went first.

Others rode alongside the wagon train as skirmishers, a little way out from the road so as to flush out anybody hiding in the woods and fields. Another bunch came along behind.

There was about a dozen wagons in the train, most often pulled by teams of six horses. I was the only one with a mule team. The horse teams looked mighty handsome, but I wouldn't swap 'em for our mules. The mules didn't need as much fodder as horses and didn't take sick so easy. A mule could do more work than a horse, too. Mules are good-hearted, and willing to do their share. You couldn't help liking them.

We headed out of Stanardsville on the turnpike, aiming for Gordonsville about twenty miles away. It'd take us a long day to get that far. Then we'd take another turnpike to a place called Louisa Court House and from there on down to a road that ran into the James River near Richmond. Then we'd load the stuff on barges and take it into the city by the river.

We ambled along. A wagon train can't make the time that a single team can. If one team near the front runs into a problem, the whole line is held up. It's always stretching out and closing up. Being down at the end I was forever waiting, and then suddenly I'd have to fly into a trot to catch up. But I didn't mind, for there was a bunch of Mosbys right behind me.

Going slow allowed me to look around a good deal. Except for my trip to Charlottes-ville, I'd never been farther from home than Stanardsville, and it was all new and strange to me. It was exciting to see different places, always something new around each twist in the road—a kind of barn I'd never seen be-fore, a deep black lake, a couple of little boys who ran alongside the wagon giving the Rebel yell.

There were other things to see that weren't so precious nice: houses with the win-dows and doors blown out of them; barns burnt to the ground; whole groves of trees broken and splintered where cannon balls had smashed through them, leaving tall stumps sticking up like bayonets. Once we passed a scattering of dead horses lying on a distant hillside, rotting and bloated. Even from far away we could smell the rotten flesh—an ugly stink that would make you gag if you took a mouthful of it.

Along about ten in the morning it began to rain, a slow drizzle, bit by bit coming on a little thicker. I hunched down inside my clothes, trying to stay dry, but of course that wasn't any good, and after a while I gave up and drove on wet and shivering. The rain soaked into the dirt road. For those up front it wasn't too bad, but by the time the rear of the wagon train came along, the road had been trampled on by a hundred horses and rolled over by fifty big wagon wheels and it was churned into pea soup a foot deep.

The horses slipped and slid, struggling to pull the wagons through the mess. My mules did a little better. Being as they were smaller and lighter, they didn't sink in as deep as horses, and when there was a patch of level ground alongside the road, I steered them onto it and we moved along pretty good. But the wagon train was slowed way down. We'd be a good while getting into Gordonsville, and might not even make it by dark. So I just kept on going through the mud and the rain, walking alongside Regis so as to lighten her load.

The first shot came around noon. I didn't know what it was. It came from a good distance away and was muffled by the rain. It could have been a dog's bark, or a shout. I looked back at the Mosby horsemen behind us. They had their heads cocked, listening. Then there came a quick rattle and there wasn't any question anymore. The Mosbys dug their heels into their horses and shot past me toward the sound of firing. For a minute the thudding of hooves covered all other sounds, and then the Mosbys were around a bend in the road, and I could hear gunfire again, pretty steady now, pop, pop-pop, pop-pop-pop.

The wagon ahead of me came to a stop. The teamster driving it jumped up on the wagon seat and looked off down the road. I climbed up on my wagon seat to have a look. I couldn't see any fighting, not with the rain and the wagon ahead blocking my view.

I was mighty scared. I reached back into the wagon and pulled out Great-grampa's sword. I felt all trembly, my breath coming in short gasps, my legs weak. Scared as I was, I was bound and determined I wouldn't cut and run, but would make a fight of it. But how? All I had to do was wave Great-grampa's sword at a bluecoat and he'd shoot me dead.

Then what would happen to Ma and the

little ones? I dropped my arms down to my side and let the sword dangle. I'd promised Pa I wouldn't go off to fight, and then I'd lied to Ma about there being no risk, and here I was in the middle of a fight after all. I felt awful, for there was a real chance now I'd get killed, or captured, and lose the mules and wagon in the bargain. What was wrong with me? How could I have gone against my promise to Pa like that? What a blame fool I was. Oh, I'd done wrong, all right, and sticking around to wave Great-grampa's sword at a half dozen bluecoats just so's I could say I hadn't cut and run would make it worse yet.

I looked around. To the left a rocky hillside rose up from the road, the rocks slick with rain. There was no hope of getting the mules up there. I looked the other way. There were trees and brush along the road, going back about fifty feet. Through the trees I could see a field that had just been plowed. If I could get the wagon through those trees into the field, I might have a chance. There wasn't any telling what lay beyond. Maybe some little village where I could hole up. I had to chance it.

The gunfire was a lot closer now. I flung

Great-grampa's blamed sword back into the wagon, where it clattered down among the barrels of beef. Still feeling mighty shaky, I gave the trees alongside the road a quick look. In a minute I saw a place where there was a gap big enough to drive the wagon through. I jumped up onto Regis and didn't bother being polite to the mules, but gave Bridget a good crack with the whip and jerked the reins hard to turn them off the road. They heaved the wagon out of the mud, off onto the shoulder, and then we were into the woods, smashing down the brush. Just as we went in among the trees, I caught a glimpse down the road of blue uniforms—Yankees. I couldn't see how many there were—just a mess of them. But they were running through the rain in my direction, bayonets sticking out from their rifles.

It was slow going in the woods, for Bridget and the others weren't used to crashing through brush and didn't like it. But they didn't like all that banging and shouting on the road behind them, neither, and were willing enough to try, especially as I kept cracking that whip pretty hot.

Now I could see the field through the trees pretty good. Beyond it, in the distance, was a white steeple. There had to be a little village over there somewhere. I gave Bridget another lick, and then I saw something else— a split-rail fence running along the edge of the field, dividing it from the trees.

Blame it! I drove the mules forward through the trees until we reached the fence. Before they even stopped, I was off Regis and onto the ground. Behind me there came a shout. I swung my head around. Through the trees and the rain I could see a patch of Yankee blue. I leapt for the fence and began to wrestle the top rail out of the posts. The shout came again. I took another look. A Yankee bluecoat was coming through the trees toward me on the run. I couldn't make him out real good, but I could see the bayonet on his rifle, all right, for he was slashing the brush out of his way with it as he came.

I forced the top rail loose from the posts, heaved it onto the ground, and began to wrestle with the next one. Then there came a shot, powerful loud. I jumped, and something slapped through the air by my head. It was too late to get through the fence. I reached into the wagon, pulled the sword out from among the barrels of beef, and turned around to face the Yankee. Now I had to fight him, no matter what Pa said. I didn't know anything about swords so I raised it over my head.

He wasn't but a hundred feet from me, but what with the trees and the darkness from the rain, I couldn't make him out too good. He wouldn't have much trouble shooting me if he wanted to. My legs felt trembly, and the sweat on my face was as thick as the rain. He kept running toward me and then he shouted, "Put down that sword, Reb, or I'll blow your damn head off."

I winced, for I could almost feel that ball smacking me in the face, and all the starch went out of me. I let the sword drop. He charged up to me, the bayonet pointed straight at me. "Now lie flat," he said.

But I hardly heard what he said, for at that moment his face came out of the shadows of the trees, and I saw he was black. My mouth dropped open and my eyes got wide. I stood staring.

"Lie flat," he said. He jabbed toward me with the bayonet.

Still shocked, I dropped to the wet, dead leaves and lay there. It didn't matter about the wetness, for I was soaked through as it was. All around guns popped, horses whinnied and shrieked. It was clear that the Mosbys hadn't driven the Federals off. We'd lost the wagon train before we hardly got started. The whole thing was finished and the Yankees, not the starving people in Richmond, would get the food we were carrying. And I was captured— and so were the mules and the wagon. And captured by a darky, on top of it.

Oh, I felt terrible sick and ashamed of myself. I lay on the wet leaves with my eyes closed, my fists clenched. "I'm sorry, Pa," I whispered into the ground. "I'm sorry. I shouldn't have done it."

The black soldier was standing over me. I figured that bayonet was about six inches from my back. "Sit up slow," he said.

I banged my fists on the ground. "Lord Jesus," I whispered into the wet leaves, "get me out of here and I'll never go against Pa again."

"Sit up."

I sat up, and gave him a look. He seemed to be about my age, and my size, too. He was wearing a regular Federal uniform—blue jacket down to his waist, light blue trousers, blue cap with a black visor. It was a shock, all right—the world turned upside down. Oh, I'd heard that the Union army was taking blacks in. There'd been plenty about it in the newspapers, saying how it was an insult to our troops to have to fight against niggers—it was beneath the dignity of a white man. Some of our soldiers said they weren't going to take any colored prisoners, neither, but would kill them on the spot. Wouldn't waste good bullets on them but would chop them up with bayonets. And from what Pa said, I guess some of them did it. They said it happened at Fort Pillow on the Mississippi after a battle there, and at other places, too. Pa said it wasn't right and our officers weren't suppose to let it happen. Besides, once word got around among the black soldiers that they might be chopped up if they surrendered, they'd fight to the death, which would only make it worse for us. But I could understand why our troops would do it, for it *was* beneath the dignity of a white man to have to fight darkies as equals.

So I'd known there were darkies in the Union army. But I didn't have no idea they were regular soldiers dressed in uniforms, drilling and carrying guns just like white soldiers. I pictured them in my mind dressed the way I generally saw them at home—barefoot, tattered shirt, old pair of pants with patches on the seat. I didn't picture them marching into battle in drill formation, neither, or carrying guns; I saw them charging in a howling mob with shovels, picks, and clubs. The sight of this darky standing over me just didn't fit anything I knew about colored folks since I was big enough to know anything.

"Git up," he said.

Taking orders from a darky was another shock, especially one my own age. It was just the strangest thing, for I'd never heard a darky even speak back to a white person, much less give them orders. I wondered: would he back down if I yelled at him? Great-grampa's sword was lying where I dropped it, just a couple of feet away. What would happen if I snatched it up and lunged at him with it? Did he really know how to shoot that rifle? I reckoned maybe he could: darkies weren't smart enough for much, which is why they had to have white people over them to tell them how to do things, but it didn't take a whole lot of brains to shoot a rifle, especially when you were only five feet away. I might get to him with the sword before he shot me, but I doubted it. So I stood up.

He looked me over. The sounds of fighting were dying out now, with only a pop-pop here and there, although a couple of horses were still shrieking out on the road. "Looks like I done captured me a Reb," he said. He looked mighty pleased with himself. "I wish my pappy could see me—it'd do his heart good."

I stared at him, but I didn't say anything. I hated having him lord it over me.

"Hop up on the mule," he said.

"Don't push me," I said.

He shoved the bayonet at me. "You heard me. Climb up there on that there mule."

My temper got away from me. "I'm not taking orders from no nigger," I shouted.

He poked the bayonet toward me, so the point of it flicked my shirt. "You're taking orders from this nigger. Git up on that there mule."

I didn't say anything. Would he really stab me?

"Git up there. I'd just as lief run you through where you're standing as look at your ugly face all the way back down to City Point. Save a lot of trouble and the expense of shipping you north to a prison camp."

Well, I was stuck. If I didn't do what he said, he would run me through. He'd have to, for he couldn't just turn and walk away. He'd leave my body here in the woods to rot and stink like the horses I saw awhile back. That'd be the end of me, and Ma and the little ones would suffer for it. They'd never know what happened to me. I had to get back to them with the mules and wagon. That was the only thing that mattered now, and if it meant taking orders from a nigger, why, I'd have to do it. If I stayed alive, maybe I'd find a way to escape, somehow. So I clambered up on Regis. The darky picked up Great-grampa's sword and climbed into the wagon. "Head on out to the road," he said.

I turned the mules around and started them off through the woods the way I'd came. I took a quick look over my shoulder. The black soldier was sitting on the wagon seat with his rifle draped over his lap more or less pointed at the middle of my back. With his free hand he was slashing the sword around in the air.

"That's my great-grampa's sword," I said.

"It ain't your grampa's anymore."

I looked away from him so I wouldn't lose my temper. A few minutes later we were back on the road, about at the spot where I'd jumped into the woods a half hour before.

Oh, my, it was a different-looking place. The wagon that had been in front of me was turned over on its side, and the horses were all down, still in the harnesses, two of them dead with their tongues hanging out of their mouths, a couple of them whinnying and struggling to get up, but too tangled in the harness to get on their feet. A couple of bodies lay in the road farther along—teamsters, for they had on regular clothes instead of uniforms. Still farther in the distance a wagon stood with the traces empty, the horses gone, taken away by the Yankees. Beyond it were some more bodies tangled up with a couple of dead horses. One of them was dressed in blue, I was glad to see. And milling around everywhere were Yankee soldiers—most of them darkies on foot, but a few white officers on horseback among them, for even the Yankees had enough sense to realize you needed white people to tell the darkies what to do.

As we came onto the road, a couple of black soldiers trotted over to the wagon. "Hold it." I reined in the mules. The black soldiers peered in. "Well, looks like Private Turner got hisself his own driver."

It was a shock to hear a darky called by a last name. I never hear of such a thing before—always heard them called nothing but Amos, Sam, Henry. I turned and looked back. Private Turner was grinning to beat the band. "Gonna see what it feels like to set up here high and mighty while this buckra takes the orders."

"Whatcher got in them barrels, Reb?" one of the others said.

I knew I ought to be polite, but my feelings were on the boil. "See for yourself."

He stared at me. Private Turner said, "This here buckra's got hisself a mouth."

"Whyn't you poke 'um with that there sword, Private Turner, to teach 'um some respect."

I felt something sharp stick me between

the shoulder blades. "All right," I said. "It's barrels of beef."

"That's better," the one on the ground said. "Now you jist hop off'n that there mule and set them barrels on the ground. When you get 'em outten there, theys a couple of wounded fellas down the road. Heave 'um in the wagon and take 'um into City Point with you."

That was the worst part. While that black soldier, Private Turner, sat up there in the wagon playing with Great-grampa's sword, I wrestled the barrels out of the wagon, sweating and grunting in the rain. My feelings were still mighty hot and I came near to saying the devil with it, I'd go for him, even if I got killed for it. But I didn't, for in the end Ma and the little ones would suffer for it. So I emptied out the wagon, climbed back on Regis, and started the mules off again, skirting along the edge of the road to go around the bodies. I don't know as I'd ever felt worse in my life, not even right after Pa died. I'd busted my promise to Pa, and it'd come out just the way he figured it would. How would I ever get back home? Oh, how I wished I'd never heard about this wagon train. Oh, how

I wished I hadn't lied to Ma about it being safe. It felt awful, for wish as I might, I couldn't turn things around again.

We came to the wounded men. They were lying by the side of the road, propped up against trees, breathing deep, like they were having a hard time getting enough air. "Haul them two fellas over here," Private Turner said.

I was getting a little more used to taking orders from him, but not a whole lot. I still got a flash of anger from it, but I climbed off Regis and waded through the mud and the rain to the wounded teamsters. As I came up, one of them raised up his head and I saw it was Jeb Wagner. He sucked in a big swallow of air. "Hello, youngster," he gasped out. "Did you kill any of them bluecoats with your sword?"

I felt too miserable even to blush. One of Jeb's shoulders was all torn up, the cloth of his shirt mashed into the flesh and dripping blood. "They told me to put you in the wagon and take you to City Point. Maybe they'll put you in a hospital there."

"I don't know, youngster. Maybe it'd be better to die here than be bumped and bounced around in that wagon for three days just so's I can die at City Point."

"Maybe you won't die. Maybe they'll fix you up there."

He shook his head. "I got my doubts." But he struggled to his feet. I got under his good shoulder and helped him through the mud and up into the wagon.

The other fella was considerable worse off. He had a bayonet cut across his stomach that was bleeding pretty bad. I ripped up his shirt and tied it around his middle to stop the bleeding. It hurt him something awful to walk, and he kept moaning as we picked our way through the mud to the wagon. But I got him in. Then I climbed up on Regis.

Chapter Six

They formed us up into a little wagon train—just four or five wagons that hadn't got damaged and whatever horses that had been saved. Off we went for City Point. The black soldiers formed up in front and behind us, and alongside as well. There was a good many more of them than we'd had of Mosbys. It wasn't any wonder they drove us off.

The rain was slackening off some, and with a little luck the sun would break through. In a couple of hours I'd be dry and a lot more comfortable. But it would be a good while before the road was dry and level again.

City Point was on the James River, not far from Petersburg. Petersburg was set along the Appomattox River. The Yankees had got it surrounded on the other three sides and were holding it under siege, hoping to starve our troops out. Petersburg was an important place—lots of factories there making war supplies, lots of railroad lines going in and out. The Appomattox ran into the James and then out to sea. Half the transportation routes from the South up to Richmond ran through Petersburg: if the Yankees took it, Richmond wouldn't hold out for long. Least that's what it said in the papers.

One of the wagon wheels rolled over a rock buried in the mud and gave the wagon a good bump. Both of the wounded men let out moans. It made me feel bad. I wished I could give them a smooth ride, but there wasn't any way to do it, not on that muddy road filled with sink holes. They were going to be moaning all the way to City Point, and they'd probably be sicker for it. I resolved to pay close attention to the road, so as to spare them fel-

las as much as possible. That is, if I could persuade Bridget to see it my way: she wasn't
mean, just ignorant, and didn't know she was
killing them fellas when the wagon rolled over
a bump. But the rain had about quit, and a
pale yellow sun was filtering down. With luck
the road would be hard in a day. It'd still be
bumpy, but not so bad as now.

I began to think about going to a Union
prison. I'd heard a lot about them, for soldiers
who'd got out of them told stories to the
newspapers. They were pretty terrible—jam-
packed with prisoners sleeping in cabins or
even tents all through the winter. Or if they
were lucky, locked in some kind of old factory
or warehouse, where you had to take turns
crowding around the stove to stay warm. The
food was the worst kind of stuff—rotten potatoes, hardtack with maggots in it, and not
much else. Worse, there was a good chance
you'd take sick and die. They died like flies in
them prison camps: froze to death, starved, or
died of the chills and fever. Every morning
they'd carry bodies out, dozens and dozens of
them. Oh, they were terrible places, all right.

We had our own prison camps, that was

true. But ours weren't near as bad as the Northern ones. At least that's what our newspapers said.

It plain hurt to think about being sent off to one of them prison camps, for as far as Ma and Sam and Sarah went, it was the same as if I was dead. Ma'd have to cut the wood, plant, hoe, and all the rest. I just didn't see how she could do it herself. How was she going to plow and haul wood up from the wood-lot without the mules? Probably Mr. Reamer'd come up and plow for her, but that wasn't going to get the wood out, the corn planted, the hay cut, raked, and brought up to the barn. The truth was, she couldn't. Of course, with no mules to feed, she could trade the hay off to somebody who still had live-stock to feed—get some wood cut, or some such in the bargain. But it wouldn't hardly be enough. There was no way around it: they were going to be hungry and cold next winter, and likely to take sick themselves. Making it worse, they wouldn't know if I was alive or dead, and would be down on their knees praying for me morning and night, the way we did for Pa.

Picturing them on their knees shivering

and hungry, praying for me, I blame near busted out crying. I didn't deserve no praying over. I didn't deserve no better than to be stuck away in a Northern prison to eat rotten potatoes and shiver with the cold. I whispered, "Forgive me, Pa, I was a blame fool." Then I said the Lord's Prayer a couple of times in hopes it would ease my conscience, but it didn't.

The only thing that would do that, I reckoned, would be to get back home safe with the mules and the wagon. I had to get away; I just had to. I took a quick look over my shoulder at Private Turner. He wasn't paying attention to me but was looking around at the sights. There was a good deal to look at—a capsized wagon by the side of the road, a house with one side of it blown off, so's you could see the rooms upstairs and down—sofa, bed, carpets, piano, pictures on the wall. Maybe while he was observing the sights I could catch him off guard, grab Great-grampa's sword away from him and stab him with it. Then what? I could try to make a break for it, but there were Federals all around the wagon and they'd shoot me dead before I got ten feet.

What was the chance of the Mosbys coming back with extra men and rescuing us? I gave it some thought. It seemed reasonable. They wouldn't have liked it none getting beat that way, and most likely would want to get even. Maybe they were out there that very minute rounding up reinforcements to save us. Or maybe we'd bump into a passel of some other Southern troops who'd chase the darky Federals off. This war wasn't laid out neat and clean, with us over here and them over there and a line down the middle. Instead both armies were chasing each other around, like two dogs in a fight trying to get an angle on the other. Either side might pop up anywhere. So there was always a chance of bumping into our own troops.

But it wasn't nothing I could count on. The Mosbys might be itching for revenge; on the other hand, they might have done all the fighting they cared for right then and didn't want nothing but to hole up in front of a nice fire and dry off. If anybody was to save me, it would probably have to be me. I'd just better put my thinking cap on and come up with something. Otherwise I'd spend the rest of my life with Pa hanging over my shoulder, looking grim and sorrowful.

But I couldn't come up with any plan, and after a while I got tired of thinking. To take my mind off it, I took out my little book of psalms and began to read them in a soft voice to myself. "The Lord is my shepherd, I shall not want. He maketh me to lie down in green pastures. He leadeth me beside the still waters . . ."

"Who you talking to?" Private Turner said suddenly.

I turned around again. He'd left off playing with Great-grampa's sword and had stuck it in his belt. It made me mad to see it there. "I wasn't talking to anybody. I was reading the Psalms."

He stared at me for a minute. Then he said, "Someday I'm gonna learn to read. Just wait and see. Soon as the war is done and the colored is all free, I'm gonna learn to read."

"Why would a—" I started to say, but stopped myself in time. "Don't be too sure the Yanks'll win. You haven't done it yet. You been trying to bust into Petersburg for a year now and into Richmond a lot longer than that, and you haven't done it." I got sick of looking at him with Great-grampa's sword in his belt and turned back to my Psalms again. "He restoreth my soul; He leadeth me—" I read.

Again Private Turner interrupted me. "You really readin' that? You ain't got it by heart?"

I swung around again. It was cheering me up a good deal to realize I had one over him. "Sure, I can read it. I can read anything —the Bible, newspapers, even big fat books." I stopped to see how he was taking it. "I can do sums, too, and say the times table."

He frowned. "Someday I'm gonna learn all that, too."

I was glad I was making him feel bad. "I had a lot of schooling when I was little. I studied geography and history and a whole lot of stuff. I can name the capitals of all the states and all the countries of the world, too." As soon as I said it, I wished I hadn't. I knew all the capitals once, but I wasn't sure I remembered them anymore. But then, it didn't seem likely he knew them, neither.

"All right," he said. "If you're so smart, what's the capital of New York State?"

"That's easy. New York City."

"Well, it ain't. That shows how much you know."

I didn't see how he could be right. "What is it, then?"

He didn't say anything for a minute. Then he said, "Well, it ain't New York."

"How come they call it New York, then?" I had him there and he knew it.

"Okay, Reb, what's the capital of South Carolina?"

He had me there this time. The only place I knew of in South Carolina was Fort Sumter. Everybody knew about Fort Sumter, because that's where the war started: the Yankees were holed up there and we kicked them out, and after that the war was on. It seemed like a good guess to me: they wouldn't have started the war over some little bitty place, but over the capital. I took a chance. "Fort Sumter."

He busted out laughing. "Why you don't know nothin' at all about capitals, Reb. It ain't Fort Sumter, it's Charleston. I know that because it's where my pappy got sold off to. After he sold him, Marse Stevens told us Pappy was lucky, for he wasn't going to no rice plantation in the middle of nowheres, but to the state capital."

Well, I didn't know if he was right or not. It was hard for me to believe that a darky could know anything about the state capitals, but if a white person told him, he might. To change the subject I said, "How come he got sold off?"

Private Turner shrugged. "The white massa do what he wants with the colored."

"My pa was worse than sold off. He got wounded at Cedar Creek and come home and died."

"His own fault," Private Turner said. "He shouldn't of took up arms against the Constitution."

That made me bristle, all right. I wasn't going to have some darky with no schooling and no brains tell me what the Constitution said. "You don't know the first thing about it. It's states' rights. The Constitution says plain as day that the union was put together by the states and could be pulled apart by the states. Virginia had a right to quit, and the Federals didn't have no business coming down on us the way they did."

"States' rights ain't got nothin' to do with

it. The war's about some people bein' held in bondage by other people. It's in the Bible. 'Ye are all children of God by faith in Christ Jesus.' We all the same in His eyes and no one should be set over another."

"Fat lot you know about it. You can't read the Bible and I can. It says, 'Servants, be obedient to them that are your masters.'" That shut him up, for he couldn't be sure what was in the Bible, and I could.

But it didn't shut him up for long. "The Devil can quote Scripture, Reb. It says in the Bible that God goes with the servants and will soon bring the day of jubilee. Pretty soon the North is goin' to be master of the South, and us colored is going to have you buckras steppin' mighty lively."

Oh, did that burn me. I came near to jumping off that mule and going for him. But he knew what I was thinking, for when I swung around I saw that rifle pointed dead at me. My turn would come, I was bound and determined on that.

Then we hit a sink hole in the road. The two wounded fellas groaned, and I turned back to the road, so as not to bounce them again. The sun was pretty strong and I was drying out some. Jeb gave a little cough. "Hey, youngster, how about reading some more of that Bible stuff. It takes my mind off things." So I began to read again, and we went on like that for quite a while until my voice got tired and I had to quit. I figured I'd read them some more as soon as my voice was rested, seeing as it made them fellas feel better. At least it made Jeb feel better; the other fella just lay there with his eyes closed, and I didn't know if he was taking anything in. Besides, it reminded Private Turner that I could read and he couldn't.

At nightfall the little wagon train pulled off the muddy road into a field. At least we were on dry ground. We circled the wagons around. The colored bluecoats put out guards to patrol the area, got their cooking fires going, and set up tents for the night. I got off Regis and stretched, glad to have a rest. Private Turner got down, too. "Don't you try to run for it, Reb," he said. "There's patrollers out there that'll shoot you dead at the first step." Off he went. I set about unhitching the mules and tethering them for the night. I took some time to clean out their hooves, too, for they'd got clogged with mud.

What would happen if I made a break for it? There was still a little light in the sky to the west. When that went, maybe I could crawl out of there and be gone before anyone knew it. It might be worth the chance. But that would mean leaving the mules and the wagon behind.

Now I could smell beef cooking—the beef I was supposed to carry to Richmond, for all I knew. It smelled mighty good. I looked around. In the dim light I could see the black faces all crowded around fires. They stuck chunks of beef on their bayonets and were holding them over the flames. Oh, my, it smelled good. I hadn't anything to eat since breakfast and had a pretty busy time of it since then. I was just about as hungry as could be. Plenty tired, too, but hungry most of all. I wondered if they meant to feed me. It didn't look like it, but they might, after they'd got themselves satisfied. I climbed up on the wagon and sat there smelling the beef and feeling sorry for myself.

Maybe I ought to try to slip away.

Maybe I ought to forget about the mules, wait until it got full dark, and then crawl away. Nobody was paying me much mind. Private Turner, he liked pushing me around, for he was a kid like me and probably didn't get much chance to push anybody around. He'd be sorry if I disappeared on him. But none of the rest were taking much interest in me. I don't think they cared a hoot if I skipped off.

Suddenly Private Turner was standing next to me. He said, "I reckon you'd like something to eat, Reb."

I hated to admit anything to him, but if I didn't I'd go hungry. "I wouldn't mind a little bite of something. Not that I care much one way or another."

"Suit yourself," he said. But he didn't leave—he went on standing there by the wagon. He wanted me to beg.

But I wasn't going to. "Well, I reckon I could manage to swaller down a little something."

"I reckon you could just choke down a nice piece of roasted beef all dripping with juice," he said.

Before I could catch myself, I licked my

lips. I was blame sorry, but I couldn't help it. "I wouldn't mind."

He didn't say anything for a minute. "Well, I tell you what, Reb. If you was to learn me to read a little, I might just be able to scrape up a nice hot chunk of beef. And a pull at a jug of cider, too."

That sure surprised me. Why in the devil would some darky, who probably wasn't smart enough for it anyway, want to learn to read? I sat there, thinking about it. I didn't much like the idea of it. In fact, you weren't supposed to teach darkies to read. There was a law on it. It just gave them big ideas. They thought it put them on a level with white folks, and it wasn't right for a white person to help in that. "Why're you so hot to learn to read? What use is reading to nig—colored folks, when like as not most of 'em won't never do anything all their lives but hoe corn and pick cotton?"

"That's that meaning of it, right there," he said. "I sure ain't gonna spend the rest of my life plowing, planting, and picking for somebody else's table. I done that since I was six years old. I'm gonna get some learning and kiss that old plow good-bye for good."

I still didn't see how any darky had enough brains to learn to read. I knew I better not put it that way, though, no matter what my feelings were. I said, "I still don't see the use of it. You got to plow to eat."

"Mebbe not," he said. "Mebbe I be a schoolteacher when I grow up."

Well, I near busted out laughing. It was the funniest thing I ever heard of. Of course, I couldn't laugh, except to myself. Besides, that beef smell was tickling my nose. I could near taste it, and I licked my lips. "I still don't see the use of it."

"Suit yourself, Reb. You won't learn me, I get somebody else."

Then an idea began to creep into my head. What if I pretended to teach him to read? What if we sat around going over my Psalm book and I showed him a few words? Why, we were bound to get to joking around a little, and by and by we'd get friendly. Then I'd tell him I was going to take the mules off to water them in some little stream we were passing—some kind of excuse like that. And then I'd make a break for it.

Besides, I didn't have to teach him right,

did I? How would he know? "All right. I'll do it." I wasn't in any rush, though. All I wanted right then was a piece of that beef. "Too dark now," I said. "I'll start to learn you when we get a chance tomorrow."

Chapter Seven

I slept in my wagon alongside the two wounded men. It was pretty crowded with three of us in there. They groaned and kicked around all night. But it was better than sleeping on the cold ground and waking up covered with dew.

We got going again before sunup and traveled all morning along rutted roads. The ground was drying now, and pretty soon instead of mud there'd be dust. But at least we were warm and dry.

Around noon we came to a place where a creek ran through the woods by the road. It was a chance to water the animals, so we swung off there. Private Turner went off to get us some food. I unhitched the mules, led them out into the water, and let them drink. They lay down on their backs in the stream, wriggling and kicking their feet around, having a great time of it. Mules just love to scratch their backs. After a few minutes Private Turner came back with some chunks of bread and dried apples. "Here," he said. "Now we got time for a reading lesson."

I took a piece of bread and chewed off a hunk. "Soon as I finish this I'll get my Psalm book." I wasn't going to be in no hurry about it.

"No," he said. "I want you to learn me this." He took a bitty piece of paper out of his breast pocket and handed it to me.

It was a story clipped out of a newspaper. The headline was *"ADDRESS OF PRESIDENT LINCOLN AT GETTYSBURG BATTLEFIELD."* "No, I'm not going to learn you this."

"You got to. I seen to it you got something to eat."

"I never agreed to read this." I shook the paper at him. "Here. Take it before I lose my temper and crunch it up."

"You better not, Reb." He grabbed hold of his rifle like he was going to unsling it from his shoulder. He was serious, all right. That little scrap of paper meant a whole lot to him. Abraham Lincoln was like Jesus Christ to him, and that piece of paper was holy, like a Bible or a gold cross was to some people. If I crunched it up, I didn't doubt but what he'd try to stick me for it. The whole thing brought me up short. Could a darky have holy feelings about things? I never knew any darkies real well, for nobody up on our mountain kept any. But I'd dealt with 'em often enough. Some of the people down in the valley I teamstered for kept slaves, and they'd help load up the wagon; and there was likely to be slaves working in the mills and warehouses where I delivered goods. I got to know some of 'em a little. It never seemed to me they had much by the way of holy feelings. They were always chattering and joking—never took anything serious as far as I could see. Even in their churches they sang and danced like they were at a party.

And here was this Private Turner all serious and holy about that bitty piece of paper. It didn't make sense; it didn't fit. The only explanation for it I could think of was that he was different from the rest of them. Of course, if he had any brains, he'd know there wasn't nothing holy about a speech by a cheap politician like Abe Lincoln. But he didn't, and to him that paper was holy.

Still, I could see that if I was to cozy up to Private Turner, I had to go along with him. "All right. If that's what you want."

He gave me a hard look. "That's what I want."

We sat down in the sunny side of the wagon, next to each other, so we could both look at the speech, munching on the bread and dried apples. I tell you, it felt might funny to sit side by side with a colored Yankee soldier, like we were old pals having a grand time together. "Okay, first you got to learn your *ABC*'s." I figured I'd tell him *A* was *M*, *T* was *J*, and so on.

"I know that part. I learned it."

That was another surprise. "How'd you do that?"

"Back home they had a school for the

white children, just a little old tumbledown place. I took to sneakin' off there when I could. It was raised up a foot off the ground, for the snakes, the way a lot of them places is. I squeezed underneath it and lay there listening to the old missiz teachin' them kids."

"Weren't you scared of those snakes?"

"Naw. I had an old snake skin in a little pouch tied round my neck, that I got from a conjure lady. Snakes won't go near nobody with one of them things."

It was just like the colored to believe something like that. But you never knew about such things—sometimes they were true. "So. Go on. How'd you learn the letters?"

"I lay there quiet as could be and took it all in. Then one day I had a sneezin' fit. The missiz thought a skunk or a possum got under the school. She came out with a broom and poked me out of there. She whaled me with that broom all the way back to the house, where I was supposed to be hoein' the radishes. So I never got no further than the ABC's."

One way around teaching him, I could see, was to keep him onto some other subject. "Where's back home?"

He sort of waved to the north. "Back up the Shenandoah Valley."

"Where exactly? I'm from over that way."

"Just an itty-bitty place. Up toward Stephens City."

"I've been up there, teamstering." It was funny to think we were almost neighbors.

"Spent my life hoein' tobaccy and getting my tail whipped with a birch switch and never had no hope of nothing else."

I wouldn't have liked that very much myself, knowing I was to spend the rest of my life hoeing tobacco. But of course the darkies didn't suffer from it as much as white folks would. "My pa whipped me when I did something wrong," I said. "Once I stole five cents out of his coat to buy candy with. He whipped me till I hollered so loud Ma made him stop. I never did that again."

"I bet he didn't draw no blood. When I got whipped, Marse Stevens generally kept at it until he cut my skin. Eat standing up for a week after that."

"Pa never wanted to hurt me, only give me a good stinging, so's I learned my lesson."

"Gettin' whipped by your pappy ain't the

same as by your massa. Pappy whipped me, too, when I got uppity, but he didn't draw no blood. Marse Stevens drew blood on *him*, you can bet. Took three men to hold him down, and Marse Stevens whipped him until his back wasn't nothin' but blood and meat. By the time Marse Stevens sold him off to South Carolina, his back was so shiny from scars you could near see your face in it."

"Probably he did something wrong and deserved it."

He stuck his face in mine. "Don't you ever say nothin' about my pappy or I'll kill you dead where you sit."

I jumped. I'd never seen a darky lose his temper with a white man like that. Of course, I wouldn't like it, neither, if somebody said my pa deserved a whipping, but I didn't expect Private Turner to feel the same as me.

I wasn't about to apologize. I'd never apologize to a darky even if he was to shoot me for it. But I could see where it would only be Christian to tone it down a little. "Most likely your master was too hard with his colored. Some of 'em are." I decided to get on a subject less likely to rile him up. "Why're you so all-fired-up to learn to read? I never heard of a nig—darky who could read." You take an ordinary white boy, you practically had to beat him to get him to learn anything. And here was a darky you had to beat to keep him from learning.

"Why, what you talkin' about, Reb? Plenty of colored can read, and write books, too. You take Frederick Douglass, he wrote a wheelbarrow full of books. He says it ain't goin' to do the colored no good just to be free. We got to be educated, too, like the buckra, else we'll spend our lives behind a plow lookin' at the wrong end of a mule."

That took me all right, for it was just what Pa said: a lot of the fellas he soldiered with couldn't read nor write and would spend their lives behind the plow. Most likely this here Douglass must of overheard some white man say it first. It was probably true that there were some black folks you could teach things to. Just by the law of averages there was bound to be. But from what I'd seen of the colored—the way they talked and such— it didn't seem likely that you could teach most of them very much. I was curious to know how much Private Turner actually knew. "How'd you learn the letters if you were under the school and couldn't see 'em?"

"Oh, she had 'em writ on the blackboard. Whenever I got a chance I'd slip off there and peek at 'em through the window. Course I didn't know which end of the *ABC*'s come first —the end toward the window or the end toward the stove. I just guessed at it and picked the end by the window, and learned the whole thing, scratching out the letters in the dirt. I got it memorized good, and then one day I saw little Marse Richard, who wasn't but seven then, writing his name in the dirt the same as I done, and saying the letters out loud to show off to his ma, and I seen I'd learnt the whole thing backward. Oh, it made me feel mighty blue, all that work for nothing. But I set about clearin' it out of my head and learned it right."

One surprise after the next. This fella wasn't as stupid as most of 'em. It was hard for me to believe there was a darky in the world that had any brains. But maybe he was lying. I pointed my finger to the word *brought* in that speech of Lincoln's. "What's those letters?"

He put his finger down next to mine and I pulled my hand away. *"B-r-o-u-g-h-t.* What's that say?"

I began to feel kind of uneasy. He was going to be harder to fool than I reckoned on, and would be mighty riled up if he caught me at it. But I wasn't going to help a darky set himself up as good as a white man. "Oh, that means broke," I said.

He put his finger under the word again, and worked the sound of it out for himself. "Bro-ugg-t." He looked at me. "That's mighty funny. You sure you got that right?"

I began to feel hot. He was on to me, but for the wrong reason. "No, that's right. Only the *h* doesn't count."

He gave me another funny look. How come the *h* don't count?"

He had me stumped. "It just doesn't, is all. In words there's a lot of letters that don't count. Like, you take *neighbor,* any fool would think it was spelled *n-a-y-b-o-r.* But it isn't, it's *n-e-i-g-h-b-o-r,* only the *g* and *h* don't count. Same as in *weigh.* There's a *g* and *h* in there that don't count, neither. Or *freight.*"

"Why don't they just leave *g* and *h* out'n the list if they don't count?"

"Oh, sometimes you need 'em. You take *ghost*. The *g* sounds there, it's only the *h* that's a waste."

He scratched his head. "All right, keep the *g* but let the *h* go if it ain't no use."

"No, you can't do that. You need the *h* for *through. Tha-roo*," I explained. "In that one you don't need the *g*." I frowned. "Of course, there's an *h* at the end you don't need, nei-ther."

He stared at me. "You sure you got this right?"

Well, I did have. I was confusing him more by telling him the truth than by teaching him wrong. "Oh, it's right. You can ask any-body."

He shook his head. "It's the most mis-chievous thing I ever come up against. Now lemme ask you this. How do you know when they count and when they don't count?"

I was stumped again. "There isn't any rule for it. You just got to learn 'em, is all."

Luckily, just then the Federals started hollering that it was time to get back on the road. Private Turner took the newspaper clip-ping from me, put it carefully in his breast pocket, and buttoned the pocket. I hitched up the mules, climbed onto Regis, and pulled onto the road with the little wagon train, feeling kind of relieved that I'd got out of the reading lesson safe.

I was still worried about bouncing those poor wounded fellas too much. Every once in a while Jeb would ask for a drink of water, and I'd give him some from my bottle. He didn't drink much of it, just wet his mouth a little. I'd ask him how he was doing and he'd try to give me a wink and say he was fine. But he wasn't. The other fella wasn't doing even that good. He had his eyes closed most of the time and mumbled a good deal. It seemed to me like it would be kinder to set him off someplace in the sun by the side of the road and let him die in peace, but you weren't supposed to do that.

That night we fitted in another reading lesson while we ate. I saw pretty quick I couldn't tell him every word wrong, for I'd never be able to keep track of it myself. I had to teach him wrong just here and there, whenever I figured I could get away with it. When he got suspicious and sounded out the word, I'd explain it was another case of where some of the letters didn't count. Pretty soon I'd either escape, or get sent north to a Union prison camp. Either way I'd be shet of him, and it wouldn't matter to me when he found out I'd been teaching him wrong. He was bound to find out sooner or later. After that he wouldn't trust anything I taught him and would have to start all over again. Maybe he would learn to read and maybe he wouldn't, but if he did it wouldn't be my fault.

Still, it was risky teaching him wrong, and I tried to get out of the lessons as much as possible. Anyway, the main idea for me was to get friendly with him, so it came natural to get off Lincoln's blame speech and ramble on to something else. Like, the speech began off, "Four score and seven years ago." Naturally, Private Turner wanted to know what in tarnation *four score* meant. So I explained that a score was twenty, so four score was eighty and four score and seven was eighty-seven. I could see he was mighty impressed with the way I toted that up.

"What's it mean?"

"Lemme see," I said, looking for a way to ramble off. I looked at him. "When's this here speech from?"

"A couple of years ago. Captain Bartlett

read it out to us at formation one day. I asked him if I could keep it."

"Well, all right," I said, figuring on impressing him some more. "Lincoln gave this speech in 1863. So 'four score and seven years ago' is . . . is . . ." I picked up a stick and scratched the numbers in the dirt to subtract them. "It's 1776. Why, blame it, that's the meaning of the thing. He's talking about when the Declaration of Independence was signed."

"What's that?"

"Why, that's the most important thing that ever was. It's when we declared we was free of the British, and fought the Revolution over it. Same as the South declared it was free of the Federal government."

"Same as Lincoln declared the colored was free of the masters," he said.

"That isn't the same thing at all as the Declaration of Independence."

He thought about it for a minute. "Now, Reb, awhile ago you was sayin' this here war was about states' rights and the Constitution. Now you got the Declaration of Independence in there, too."

The truth was, I was getting myself all tangled up. Why had Lincoln thrown that blame *four score* in there? "That's just Lincoln's way of putting it. I didn't say he was right." I decided to get off it. "Anyway, that's what four score and seven means."

He nodded. Then he said, "Whyn't he just say eighty-seven straight out, instead of confusin' folks?"

"It's like the way a preacher talks. It sounds more noble if you come at a thing sideways instead of hitting it straight on." Then I said, "Did Marse Stevens let you go to service when you were back home?" and we rambled off on the subject of preachers and what kind of church he went to, and such. Some of it was mighty interesting. They weren't allowed to have a regular church, he said, but one of the old slaves set himself up as a preacher. On Sundays all the slaves would come together in a patch of ground by the cabins and old Deacon Jack would holler 'em. Then they'd have a ring shout. That was the best part, he said. "You ain't allowed to dance at a meetin', so you got to keep both feet on the ground while you go round and round. Oh, they's some mighty powerful singin' at some of them shouts, the folks all clapping their hands. Some 'em ketch the spirit. They eyes roll back and they speak in tongues. It sounds like real talk, but not so's you nor me could understand it."

"It happens to white folks, too," I said. "At camp meetings. Pa didn't hold with it, and we never went to no camp meeting, but the Reamer boys over to Conrad's Store did, and they told me about it. They said a couple of women started talking real funny and finally just keeled over. But I never heard of no dancing."

"It ain't dancin'. You ain't allowed to dance. You got to keep your feet on the ground all the while you go around—shuffle 'em along." And he stood up and showed me. Oh, it was mighty interesting, and as much as I could I got us off that blame speech and rambling on to other things.

I slept in the wagon again that night. It wasn't much of a place for sleeping, for Jeb thrashed around in his sleep a good deal and the other one mumbled near continuous the whole night, like he had something big on his mind and had to get shet of it. But there was a good side, too, for some warmth came off of them and I wasn't near as cold as I'd have been sleeping alone.

Along toward dawn, when the sky was just leaving off being dark, it began to grow colder. I shivered and tried to curl up into a ball to stay warm, but the wounded fellas didn't leave enough room to curl up in. My teeth were chattering, and after a little bit I reached out my hand to touch the fella who was doing all the mumblin', in hopes he'd shift himself. Suddenly I realized he wasn't mumbling anymore. I came full awake, sat up, and bent forward to take a good look at him. A shiver went through me, but not from the cold. I touched his face. His skin was cold. I jerked my hand back. I'd been sleeping with a dead man. I leapt out of the wagon as fast as I could move. To think I'd been lying right there next to him when his spirit rose out of him and sailed off to Heaven. I peered in over the side of the wagon. "Jeb," I whispered, although there wasn't no need for quiet.

He turned his head a little. "That you, youngster?"

"That fella, he's dead."

Jeb coughed a little. "Some fellas has all the luck," he said.

Chapter Eight

We went along mighty slow for a couple more days. The Yankees didn't know the country: a few times we made wrong turnings and had to backtrack for two or three hours. Things would happen, too. We had to take time to bury my dead fella, and we hardly got going when a wheel fell off a wagon and had to be fixed—it was always something like that.

As far as I was concerned, the slower the better, for once we reached City Point I was likely to get shipped off north. I had to escape before then, that was certain. But I wasn't sure I'd got Private Turner fetched along to where he'd let me go off alone to water the mules, or some such. I spent a lot of time thinking about how I would manage that—tell him Bridget had come down with the colic and needed to graze on a special kind of herb I saw growing back a ways, that I saw a big beehive I could reach if I drove the wagon under the branch and stood up on the seat. But none of these ideas was any good.

I didn't have trouble getting his attention, though, for every time we stopped to rest he wanted to go at reading. What's *dedicated* mean, what's *hallowed ground*, and such. To be honest, I wasn't sure myself what a lot of it meant, which was a good thing, for it allowed me to learn him wrong by mistake, instead of on purpose. So I said that *dedicated* meant they was serving refreshments after the speech, and that it was *harrowed ground*, meaning that the earth was all tore up on account of the battle.

But I understood the words, "All men are created equal" all right, and I wasn't about to learn him that. "All men are created *eagles,"* I said. "Like, everybody's got the same chance to fly up to Heaven."

He nodded his head. "I knowed that. It's out of the Scripture. Deacon Jack hollered it out a good deal—'They that wait upon the Lord shall renew their strength; they shall mount up with wings as eagles.'"

Generally speaking, though, I was able to twist things around so's we'd get off that wretched speech and ramble down a side path. Like, one time I asked him how come he was Private Turner instead of Private Stevens —most darkies didn't have no last name, and if they needed one, they usually were given the name of their master.

"It was when I 'listed up," he said. "I couldn't join unless I had two names. They said I should take Stevens, but I wouldn't, not after the way the old marse whipped us. So I taken Turner, from Nat Turner."

I knew who Nat Turner was—a slave that got up a rebellion among the other slaves down in Southampton. They murdered a lot of white folks, but he got caught and they hung him. It hit me as mighty uppity for a darky to take the name of a murderer—he dassn't have done it before the war. But I didn't say so, for we was supposed to be friendly. So I said, "What did they call you before?"

"Cush is my real name. My pappy give it to me. It's from scripture. Cush was the son of Ham and was King of Ethiopia and the pappy of Nimrod, the mighty hunter." I decided I'd call him Cush. It suited a darky a whole lot more than Private Turner.

"When did you enlist, Cush?"

"Right after I run off."

"Were you in any of the fighting?"

"Naw," he said. "They use the colored for work details, mostly. Teamstering and sech. We been hauling stuff up to the front. That there battle, where I caught you, was the onliest fight I was ever in."

So he didn't know much more about war than I did; except, of course, he'd been up to the front and seen it there. "Some colored was in the fighting?"

"Oh, they sure was. Butler's Louisiana Native Guard Third Regiment beat the tar out of you Rebs at Port Hudson."

It was a hard thing to believe, that Southern soldiers could be beaten by the colored, but I reckoned it could happen if there was three or four colored to each of our men.

That night we pulled into a field beside an old farm that had seen some fighting. The house was half burnt—the roof gone and one wall down—but the barn was still standing. We circled the wagons and some of the Federals went off to see if the barn had any hay for sleeping. Cush went with them. I unhitched the mules and curried them. I was feeling pretty sorry for myself. Just about then Ma and Sam and Sarah would be sitting by the fire, Ma reading aloud from the Bible, all nice and cozy and warm. They wouldn't be worrying about me yet, for I'd only been gone for seven days and they wouldn't expect me back for ten. Oh, I came near to crying, thinking of them cuddled up close in front of the fire.

I finished currying the mules and went back to the wagon. Jeb was propped up on one elbow. "Hey, youngster," he said in a low, hoarse voice. "You got any water?"

I was always careful to fill my bottle when we stopped to water the livestock. I climbed up into the wagon and knelt down beside him so's I could hold the water bottle to his lips. He took a few sips. Then he said, "Listen, youngster, you know where I live?"

"Stanardsville?"

"Just outside, on the road toward Harrisonburg." He swallowed a little more water. "I got a feeling I'm finished. I ain't gonna make it to City Point. I got a brother back home. I want you to git word to him what happened. Otherwise nobody'll ever know. I don't want to die and not have nobody know."

"Maybe you won't die. Maybe you'll get better."

He shook his head and took another sip of water. "My legs is growing cold. That's the way it takes you. I seen a couple of fellas go this way. They both said their legs was growing cold." He sipped more water, and choked a little. "Now I know these here Yanks'll just bury me by the road in five minutes like they done with that other fella. Do me a favor, youngster. Put a couple of big rocks on top of me so's the dogs won't dig me up."

"Maybe you won't—"

He reached out, clutched at my arm, and squeezed it hard—a lot harder than I reckoned he'd be able to. "Big rocks," he said. "Big as you can drag over."

"All right," I said.

I didn't know if I'd be able to do it, for the Federals wouldn't be much interested in whether the dogs got him or not. But I reckoned I'd try.

He didn't say anything more, just lay there breathing hard and staring up at the dark sky. Finally he said, "Thanks, youngster." Then he began to shiver like a fever was passing through him, and a minute later he stopped breathing and lay still. The light faded out of his eyes.

It scared me all right to see Jeb die like that. I'd never seen anyone die. I'd been out in the barn when Pa died, and asleep when the other one died in the wagon. It was a big thing to see someone just give a shiver and a shake and stop breathing.

I knelt over him and pushed his eyelids closed, the way you were supposed to do. They popped right open. His skin was still warm and kind of damp, for he'd been sweating. It was strange to see those signs of life still on him—the sweat, the warmth, a couple of drops of water on his chin where he'd dribbled a little. I didn't like seeing him stare, so I tried to close his eyes again, but the blame lids wouldn't stay down. I rumpled around in his pocket, trying not to touch him any more than I had to, until I found his handkerchief. I spread the handkerchief over his face to stop him from staring, and climbed down from the wagon to tell the Federals he was dead. Then an idea came into my head. I climbed back into the wagon, and as soon as I saw Cush coming back towards me, I knelt down beside Jeb and held the water bottle to his lips, like he was still alive.

Cush came up to the wagon and peered in. "What's happening to him?"

"He's mighty thirsty. I don't think he can last."

"He looks dead already."

"He's mighty near it," I said, shifting around a little so as to block his view. Being as it was nearly dark, he couldn't see that there wasn't any bubbles rising in the water bottle.

He wasn't much interested in any of it. "There's some hay in the barn. Maybe I could sneak you in there to sleep tonight."

That caught me off guard. Blame me if he didn't think we were already friends. We hadn't been riding along together but three days. I guess it came from rambling along about how he learned his *ABC*'s and what kind of church we went to. To tell the truth, I wouldn't have minded having a friend right then. When you got down to it, he was a nice enough fella, willing to talk about things. And if he'd been white and on our side, I'd have jumped at the chance to make friends with him. To be honest, I'd have jumped at it even if he wasn't on our side. But I just couldn't bring myself to do that with a darky. Oh, I didn't mind being *friendly* with Cush, and rambling on about things; but that wasn't the same as being real friends.

The main thing, though, was: sleeping in the barn would ruin my plan. I took the water bottle away from Jeb's face and climbed down out of the wagon to draw Cush's attention away from the body. "That's mighty kind of you," I said. "But I reckon I better stay with this fella for a while in case he needs a drink of water or something. It wouldn't be right to let him die alone."

Cush took a look in the wagon. "He don't look like he'd notice if you was to leave. You sure he ain't dead?"

"Not yet. I 'spect he will be soon. I better stay with him until he goes."

Cush looked off through the circle of wagons. I could tell he was disappointed. "Suit yourself," he said.

The funny thing was, I felt bad about letting him down. I could see why he might want to be friends with me, for I was white. But just because he wanted to be my friend didn't mean I had to be his. Anybody white would have said the same. But blamed if I didn't feel bad. It was the old trouble of my feelings coming loose on their own, without no permission from me. I knew I better rein myself in, for it lowered a white person to get too friendly with a darky. Still, I didn't want to hurt him no more than I had to. So I said, "I'd like to, but I reckon I better see to this fella. I guess I didn't tell you, he's my ma's cousin. She'd never let me forget it if I left him to die alone."

"Suit yourself," he said, and walked away.

I'd hurt his feelings and I was sorry I

had to. But I was blamed if I was going to start crying over a darky's feeling, so I climbed back up into the wagon and took a look around.

It was near dark, but there was still light enough to see. The mules were tethered nearby, where I could keep an eye on them. Across the road from our camp was another field, and beyond that a woodlot. If I could get across the field with the mules and wagon and into the woods, I'd be safe. Crossing that open field was the problem. I'd have to make my break before the moon came up, for it was near full and it'd light up that field like day.

Now there was nothing to do but wait until the camp quieted down and the soldiers were asleep. I didn't much like the idea of sitting there in the wagon next to that body with the handkerchief over his face, but I had to make sure nobody got a look at him yet and told me to bury him before I was ready. So I sat there, getting hungrier and hungrier, for Cush was mad at me and wasn't about to bring me supper.

Time went along bit by bit. The Federal soldiers finished eating and bedded down. The camp got quiet. The fires flickered and burned low. I lay down in the wagon, trying to keep as far away from Jeb as I could, for I sure didn't want to touch him any more than I had to. I let a little more time roll over me, and then I sat up and looked around.

Everything was dead still except for two black soldiers standing by the last fire, leaning on their rifles. They were supposed to be walking guard duty around the edge of the camp, but we were close enough to City Point for them to think they were safe from Mosbys. I glanced out east: no moon yet. The field across the road was good and dark. Still, there was just enough starlight so anybody would see the shape of a wagon moving across it if they looked hard enough. But I didn't have a choice—I had to chance it.

I climbed down from the wagon and trotted over to the fire where the soldiers were standing. They were arguing about something in low voices the way soldiers do. "Say—"

They stopped arguing and looked around.

"That wounded fella in my wagon just died. He asked me—"

"Who're you?" one of the black soldiers said.

"One of the teamsters. Just before he died he asked—"

"That Reb we caught in Gordonsville?" I could tell from the way he talked that he wasn't one of our darkies, but came down from up north.

"Yes. He asked me special to see he was buried proper so the dogs wouldn't get him."

"Particular friend of yourn?"

"He's Ma's cousin from over to Stanardsville. He said I got a family duty to bury him right. Ma'd never forgive me if I didn't. Only I need a shovel."

The other black soldier shook his head. "Let it go till morning. He ain't going no place. He still be here."

"I doubt if there'll be time to bury him right before we break camp. I'd just as lief do it tonight. Besides, I'm not too happy about spending the night in the wagon with him."

"Sleep on the ground."

"Let him do it if he wants to, Willie," the first one said. "Save time in the morning."

"Only I need a shovel."

"Why cain't it wait till light?" Willie said.

"Let him do it, Willie."

"Oh, well." He pointed through the firelight into the dark. "Shovel in that 'ere wagon."

I got the shovel and went back to my own wagon. I hitched up the mules, working as fast and as quiet as I could. In about five minutes they were ready. I took a deep breath, grabbed Bridget by the halter, and started to walk them out of there. Oh, my, I never realized how much noise mules and a wagon could make. The wheels squeaked like blazes, the harness jingled, the hooves of the mules hitting the ground sounded like thunder.

Of course, the two guards couldn't miss it, and about two minutes later the one called Willie was running toward me from the fire, with the firelight behind him. "Hey Reb, where you think you gwine with that 'ere wagon?"

I stopped the mules. "He's too blame heavy for me to carry. I didn't want to start digging right here in the middle of camp and wake everybody up."

It was too dark for me to see the expression on his face, but the firelight was behind him and I could see his shape. He had his head cocked over to one side, suspicious.

"You got a answer for ever'thing, ain't you, Reb?"

"I figured I'd catch it if I waked everybody up with the digging."

"You making plenty noise with them mules. Where you figger on plantin' this fella?"

I pointed. "Just over there. By the road."

He didn't say anything for a minute, and I waited, my heart beating fast. "Okay. But be quick."

He turned and went back to the fire. I hustled the mules out of there as quick as I could, wishing there was some way to keep the wagon wheels from squeaking and squawking and the harness from playing tunes. In a couple of minutes we hit the road. I stopped the mules and looked back.

At that distance the fire was just a glow. I couldn't make out either of the guards— there was no telling where they were. I took a deep breath to calm myself down some. Then I tugged on Bridget's halter. We crossed the road and started through the field toward the woods beyond, singing and squawking in the night.

The ground was rough, for the field had

got plowed, but then the war had come through and they hadn't got it planted. The rough ground made the harness jingle worse, but I was getting far enough away so they might not hear it. I thought of poor Jeb sliding around in the wagon staring at the sky, for the handkerchief fell off his face as soon as we started up.

I got to the middle of the field. The woods weren't more than a hundred yards away. All I needed was a couple of more minutes and I'd be safe and on my way home.

Suddenly through the night there came a shout, and another shout and then the sound of cussing and running feet. I dropped Bridget's halter and fell to the ground, my heart racing. There came a gun shot. "Don't shoot," I shouted. "I'm right here."

Chapter Nine

It took some mighty fast talking, but in the end I convinced them I wasn't trying to escape. "I tried digging right there by the road, like I said I would, but it's all rocks there. I figured the ground'd be softer where they plowed it."

They were mighty suspicious and wanted me to show them where I'd dug by the road, but I said I couldn't remember where it was and wouldn't be able to find it in the dark. In the end the one called Willie went back to the fire, saying to the other one, "You was all hot to let the Reb bury this fella. You stay here and see he don't wander off no more."

I started digging. I wasn't feeling any too good. From now on they'd keep a closer watch on me. The chance of getting sent north to a prison camp was mighty likely, for we weren't more than a day or so from City Point. And it was kind of spooky digging a grave for a fella I knew and had been feeding water to just a little while ago. I figured some of that water was still in his stomach.

The whole thing set me to thinking. Poor Jeb. It didn't seem like he ever got much out of his life, and now it was done, and all for nothing. Why'd *he* got himself into the war? Was it just to keep the niggers in their place, the way he said? I wished I'd asked him more about it while I had the chance; though come to think of it, it wouldn't be so all-fired nice to ask a dying man if he wasted his life.

I got caught in up thinking and stopped digging. "Hurry up, Reb," the soldier said. "I wants to git some sleep."

I started digging again. I was about two feet down now, and getting tired, but I wanted to go deeper to save Jeb from the dogs. So I went on digging; and then the soldier said, "That 'ere's enough, Reb. Heave him in and cover him up."

He helped me lift Jeb out of the wagon and lay him down in the grave. "Is it okay if I say a prayer over him? I feel mighty sorry for him, for I can't see where the war was much use to him."

"Serves him right for getting into it, then."

"I don't see why."

"Plain enough to me. Anybody go out to fight to keep people slaves, serves 'em right to get shot."

"My pa says the war isn't over slavery, it's over states' rights."

The darky soldier laughed. "You tell that to a black man and see how far it takes you."

I could see that. "Well, I guess the colored would figure that way."

"I should just think they would. Tell the truth, my missus was agin it. She say no sense in gettin' mixed up in a white folks' war. Let 'em shoot each other for a change, 'stead of shooting niggers. Look what them immigrant crackers in New York done."

I knew about that, for it was in the newspapers. When Lincoln started up the draft, the Irish and I guess lots others said they weren't going to get themselves killed for the colored. They tore up New York and hung a bunch of darkies from lampposts. "My pa always said the Northerners weren't nothing but a bunch of hypocrites, for they didn't like colored any more than Southerners did, but at least we had the kindness to see they was clothed and fed."

"It's plain you ain't never been in the North, Reb. It ain't heaven up there the way some ignorant black folks down here think. But ain't nobody can sell your wife and kids away from you, and it sure beats hoeing tobaccy sunup to sundown and gettin' whipped for it in the bargain. Jist git this 'ere fella covered up."

I said the Lord's Prayer over the grave. When I got done, I picked up a handful of dirt and flung it on Jeb, the way the minister always did when he buried someone. "Earth to earth, ashes to ashes, dust to dust," I said, feeling sad and strange. "In sure and certain hope of the —" I couldn't remember the rest of it. "In sure and certain hope of — life everlasting." It wasn't right, but I reckoned it was close enough. I picked up the shovel and filled the grave in. "He wanted me to put some big stones over him so's the dogs wouldn't get him."

"I had enough o' this foolishness," the darky said. "Time for some sleep. Turn them mules around and git back over to camp." Poor Jeb. If I hadn't used him for a way to escape, I could have buried him proper like I promised. It worried me, for maybe his spirit would come back and haunt me for it. I heard of such things. And I resolved, if I ever got the chance, to find his brother over to Stanardsville and tell him where Jeb was buried. Maybe in the morning I could find out the name of the place where we were. Maybe that'd keep Jeb's spirit happy enough.

But, of course, in the morning I didn't remember to ask anyone, and by the time I did remember we were four or five miles down the road and nobody knew the answer. Maybe after the war I'd be able to come along this road somehow and would recognize the place.

I didn't get much of a chance to think about it, for Cush was on me from breakfast. "You was cuttin' for them woods. Now don't tell me you wasn't."

"I wasn't at all," I said. "I was just trying to find a soft place to dig. It's all packed hard by the edge of the road and full of rocks, for it never gets plowed there."

"That fella was dead the whole while. I thought he was. That's why you wouldn't sleep in the barn — you was plannin' on cuttin' for them woods. You was lyin' the whole time."

"I wasn't. Not at all. That poor fella was Ma's cousin and I had to bury him proper. You'd do the same if it was your ma's cousin."

"It didn't have nothin' to do with your ma's cousin," he said. "You a big liar. You was cuttin' for them woods. I trusted what you told me, and you was lyin' the whole time."

"Blame me if I can see why I'm not allowed to escape."

"There, you said it yourself. You was trying to escape," he said. "You oughtta know that Capt'n Bartlett'll pop me right into the stockade myself if I let you escape. I don't aim to get out of slavery to end up in jail."

I'd spoke too fast and outsmarted myself. It wasn't easy to push one past him. He was smarter than most darkies. "That was just an expression," I said.

"I don't care if it was an expression. Next time you be sorry," he said.

"You ran off yourself. Why shouldn't I?"

"That was different," Cush said.

"What was different about it?"

"Because slavery's agin Scripture."

"No, it isn't," I said. "I already told you that."

"How can any Christian believe in slavery when Jesus said flat-out all people was to be brothers unto each other?"

"Oh?" I said. "Well what about Genesis, where it says, 'Cursed be Canaan; a servant of servants shall he be unto his brethren.' It's clear enough—God made the colored black so's they could be told apart from whites."

"Where does the Bible say a fella ought to be whipped until his back is raw just because he took a piece of pork from a pig he'd done the work of raisin'?"

"Your pa got whipped for that?"

"Me. I got whipped for it. After Pa was sold off south."

It was a hard thing to argue. Back home

we'd hear about this one or that one who was hard on his slaves, but the way people put it, it wasn't the usual thing. People said most masters were too soft on their slaves and didn't beat them near enough, for darkies were lazy, would steal anything that wasn't tied down, and would eat you out of house and home if you didn't watch them close. People said most masters would be a sight better off without slaves, but only allowed them to stay out of kindness, for darkies didn't have the brains to take care of themselves if they was turned loose.

But I could see now that was only one side to it. I never asked a darky how they felt about being slaves. Was everybody back home wrong? I decided to change the subject. "How'd you manage to run off, Cush?"

"It was after Pappy was sold. Marse Stevens didn't have him to whip no more and turned hisself loose on me. I saw pretty quick that lessen I got away I was going to have a back as shiny as Pa's was. Right after that the war started. My chance come when some Union cavalry rammed through Marse Stevens' farm, foraging. They was fighting all around us and the Federals was all over the place, looking for dinner. Marse Stevens and the family went up into the woods and hid. Finally the Federals were chased out and I just run on out of there."

"How come your ma didn't go?"

"I tried to get her to, but she wouldn't. She was scairt. So I went by myself. Run up a stream a mile to throw the dogs off."

"They sent dogs after you?"

"Sure did. I could hear 'em hootin' and hollerin' way off in the distance, but they couldn't pick up the scent, on account of me running up that stream. The next day I come across a camp of Federals, and I was gone."

Well, if Cush's Marse Stevens was ripe to send dogs after a slave who'd run off, it didn't appear he was letting him stay on the farm out of kindness. But I didn't want to get into that. "What happened after you found the Federals?"

"They sent me north with a trainful of colored, up to Washington."

"You been to Washington?"

"Sure I been there," Cush said. "I seen the White House and all. We marched right past it. They said President Lincoln hisself was standing on the steps watching us go by.

Some of them said they saw him—could make him out just as plain, wearin' that stovepipe hat the way he is in pictures. If you ask me, they was seein' things, for I didn't see him and I looked mighty hard."

Here I'd never been to Richmond, and wasn't likely to get there, neither, the way things was working out, and Cush'd been to Washington. "I don't see where you were any better off if they put you in the army than you were back home."

"They didn't *put* me in no army. I joined up of my own free will."

"You didn't have to fight?"

"There ain't no law sayin' the colored got to fight. I wanted to fight. I just had to. How could I go gallivantin' around Washington, havin' a good time for myself, when Mammy and Pappy was still in slavery? I couldn't live with myself if I done that."

I could see that, for I'd have done the same myself. In fact, when you got down to it, I already did get myself in the middle of the war to get even for Pa. It was an awful lot to think about. The truth was, I never gave the darkies much thought one way or another. Up there on High Top Mountain the mules were more important to us than darkies. But now I'd got to know a darky, and I could see it wasn't simple. It made my head ache. But at least I'd led Cush off my try at escaping and into a good ramble. I had other things to think about, anyway, for when we stopped at noon to water the livestock and eat some hardtack, the soldiers were saying that with luck we'd be in City Point by nightfall.

I didn't have much time left. And now Cush was going to keep a sharp eye on me. He wouldn't take chances with me. What could I do? The idea of getting sent off to a prison camp made me just sick. What would happen to Ma and the little ones? what would happen to me? Even the poor mules—it'd go hard with them, too, for like as not the Federals would take them in the army, where there was a chance they'd be blown to bits. I hoped Pa was looking down on me, for he'd see I felt awful for what I did and wasn't taking it light. But that didn't help me to escape.

At the end of the afternoon we came down a slope to the James River. City Point wasn't far. Below us, strung across the river, was the famous pontoon bridge the papers were full of the year before. General Lee had figured that he could hold the Federals north of the James, for it would be hard for them to cross it. But practically overnight the Federals built a pontoon bridge across it, near a half mile long. I always wondered what it was like, and there it was just below me—a plank roadway running across the tops of a line of little boats anchored in the river. We went down the slope and across the bridge, the hooves and wheels making a loud drumming sound on the planks. Even though it was a Union bridge, it gave me a kind of thrill to cross it.

We reached City Point as the sun was setting. The town was set up on a bluff above the point where the James and Appomattox rivers joined up. It was all confusion, a place that the war had made, for it was mostly tents, sheds, and wooden huts thrown up in a hurry by the bluecoats. You could see the original houses scattered around in the midst of the tents and huts. Before the war City Point wasn't much of a place, but it was all abustle now. As the wagon train rolled in along the main street, I could hear the roar and clang of railroad engines, see the steam from them rising in white streams and spreading across the city. Farther along, down at the end of the street where the bluff fell off, I caught a glimpse of a couple of docks and the river full of boats—some at anchor, some sailing up or down the James, some tied up at the docks where streams of men were filing up one gangplank and down another carrying boxes, sacks, barrels of—well, I supposed it was guns, shoes, cannon balls. It made my heart sink to see it, for it was just the way Pa said—the Yankees had us beat every which way when it came to war supplies and shipping. Here it all was, ships full of it, railroad cars full of it, all coming into City Point to be thrown at Bobby Lee.

Our little wagon train swung off the main street onto a rough dirt wagon trail that wound along through the tent city. In a little bit we came to a big tent with a wood sign over the door saying 7TH REGIMENT, XXV CORPS. I knew what that was: a regiment was a thousand men and a corps was a bunch of regiments together.

The wagon train stopped, and Cush jumped off the wagon. "This here's my outfit, Reb." He pointed. "We got our huts right over there."

I sat there on Regis thinking about mak-

ing a break for it. The wagon train was breaking up. The soldiers were unloading the stuff
they captured from us, and carting it into a
sort of warehouse across the way. When the
wagons were empty, they led them off somewhere down the wagon road through the tent
city. There was a good deal of light around
from torches and lanterns, but even so I
couldn't make out where they were going
with the horses and wagons.

What if I just started the mules going,
like I was supposed to be taking them someplace, and waltzed on out of there? What
would Cush do when he came out of the regimental tent and found me gone? Would they
put him in prison for letting me get away? I
didn't know—but it might work. So I gave
Regis a kick with my heels and snapped the
reins, and that moment Cush came out of the
regimental tent with a white officer in tow.
He pointed at me. "That's him, Captain Bartlett."

I let go of the reins so it wouldn't look
like I was trying to escape again. They came
up to me. I decided to clamber down off the
mule and salute, so as to get on the officer's

good side if I could. "Where'd you come from?"

"Shenandoah Valley, sir. They sent me off with our mules and wagon to join the wagon train," I said, trying to make it sound like it wasn't my fault I was against them. "Those mules are mighty hard to control by anyone but me."

He didn't answer that. Instead he said, "How old are you, son?"

"Fourteen."

"Long way from home."

"Yes, sir."

"He was learning me to read, sir," Cush said.

Captain Bartlett went on looking at me. "Your folks Rebels?"

I thought of lying and saying that we were against secession, but I was too proud to do it. "Pa was shot at Cedar Creek and died from it."

Captain Bartlett looked grim and shook his head. "Son, do you think the whole thing is worth losing your pa for?"

"Pa said it was states' rights. He said the Yankees had no right—" Suddenly I realized

I better keep my mouth shut if I wanted to get on his good side.

He snorted. "States' rights is nonsense. The Constitution's clear enough about that. Ever read it?"

Well, the truth was, I hadn't. I guess if the war hadn't come and I'd got more schooling, I'd have read it. "Not exactly, sir."

"Read it sometime. It won't take long. It starts off with the words, 'We the people of the United States,' not 'We the states.' You can't have every state that disagrees with the laws thumbing its nose at the national government and going off by itself."

I knew I shouldn't argue with him, but he was getting my dander up. "Sir, Virginia didn't go off alone."

"It wasn't the majority, son. The majority has to rule."

"Sir, I don't see how it's different from when the U.S. busted away from England in the Revolution."

He shook his head. "Back then the states never agreed to be part of England. That was England's idea. When the United States was formed, the people in all the states agreed to take part and put the Constitution over them.

They can't choose to walk out anytime things don't suit them." He clapped his hands together. "I can't stand here arguing politics all night. Private Turner, take him down to the stockade. There's a prison train going north in a couple of days."

Chapter Ten

There it was. What could I do? I was stuck. All I could think of was the places where I could have stopped it. Thinking about it being too late is one of the awfulest feelings.

Then Cush said, "Captain Bartlett, mebbe we ought to hang on to this here Reb for a few days. He mighty handy with them mules of his. I don't know as anyone else can handle them." It took me by surprise and I held my breath, for I knew it wasn't true. Those mules could be persnickety, but they weren't all that difficult.

"Mules are mules," Captain Bartlett said. "Any good mule driver is supposed to be able to handle them."

Cush shook his head. "Not these here animals, sir. I seen for myself, for I tried to drive 'em once. Couldn't budge 'em."

Captain Bartlett gave me a look. "Is that true?"

What could I say to convince him? "I got a way with them. They're used to me. I won't say nobody else couldn't learn to manage them if you gave him time, but I reckon they'd be almighty balky to start."

"I've got more important things to do than to worry about this," Captain Bartlett said. "How are you going to keep him from running away, Private Turner?"

"We could lock him in the guardhouse when he ain't needed."

"All right, all right. But if there's trouble over it, Private Turner, it's your neck." He turned, and went back into the headquarters building.

We took the mules down to a big corral they had in the middle of the tent city, unhitched them, and turned them into the corral. We pushed the wagon into a line of other wagons up against the corral fence, and then Cush said, "Come on along with me, Reb. I got to lock you up."

But I didn't follow him right off. Instead, I stood there in the flickering light of the camp lanterns and fires, watching the yellow reflect off his black face, feeling a whole lot of different things. "Cush, how come you did that for me?"

He shrugged. "I don't know, Reb. I just didn't like to see you gettin' shoved off to no prison camp. Like to die in one of them places."

"Why would it matter to you? I'm supposed to be trying to put you back into slavery."

He shrugged again, like he was embarrassed to talk about it. "Well, you been to a lot of trouble learning me to read so's I can better myself. A lot of white folks down here wouldn't of done that."

I blushed so hot I thought my face would melt. "Oh, I didn't learn you very much. Most likely I didn't get it all right anyway. I don't know as I got the hang of all those big words myself." Oh, how I wished I hadn't taught him wrong—or even at all. What was I going to tell him when he got on to me about that blame speech again?

"No, Reb. A lot of white folks down here say it ain't right to teach a nigger to read. But you was willin'."

I didn't want to talk about it anymore. "What's the guardhouse like?"

"Old stone storehouse where they used to keep tobacco that was to be shipped out. Put bars on the windows."

"Who's in there now?"

"Just some Yank soldiers who got theirselves in trouble one way or another. They won't bother you none—got too much misery of they own."

He took me over. A couple of black guards shoved me in, gave me some hardtack, dried apples, and a worn-out blanket that smelled like a barn. I ate, rolled myself up, and the next thing I knew sunlight was streaming in the windows, even though they were barred and so dirty you could hardly see out of them. After a while Cush showed up. The guards let me out and off we went together to the corral. Already a lot of colored soldiers were milling around in the corral to chase down their teams and harness them up to the wagons lined up against the corral fence. We got my mules out, fed them, and curried them. We harnessed them up, and in a bit the order came down the line to move out. I snapped the reins and clucked a couple of times to Bridget, and off we went.

There were maybe twenty wagons in the train. We rode out through the city of tents, and down the main street of City Point toward the water. Below I could see a big wooden warehouse, the docks, the boats in the river, a string of railroad cars sitting on a siding, an engine puffing to itself, and soldiers marching up and down gangplanks of a ship tied to the docks, carrying out barrels and boxes. A ship whistle boomed, shouts and orders flew; the railroad engine puffed, gave off a shrill whistle, and then began to clang slowly along the tracks. It was mighty exciting to see, and if I hadn't been a prisoner a long way from home, I'd have enjoyed it.

The wagon train pulled down the hill and then swung around in a half circle across the front of the warehouse. Cush hopped out of the wagon. "Come on, Reb, we got to load up." I followed him into the warehouse. My, what a sight of stuff there was there: boxes, barrels, crates, and a whole lot of things lying loose—a stack of blue blankets, a heap of worn shoes, a pile of mess kits, and a mountain of old blue Federal uniforms they hadn't got around to sorting out. A colored sergeant sitting at a desk by the door to the warehouse flipped through some papers. He pointed inside. "Them kegs of powder," he said. "That's your load, gents."

Cush made a face. "Nobody likes taking powder up to the front none. The Rebs hit your wagon with a shell and it be raining mules and soldiers for a week."

We started to work, carrying the little kegs of powder out and loading them into the wagon. It was hot work, for the sun was full up now, and it was going to be a hot day. I was sweating pretty good, and after about the tenth trip out of the wagon I skipped back a ways into the warehouse, where it was cool and dark. I took a quick look around. Just ahead of me was the mountain of blue Federal uniforms. I jumped around behind it, figuring to sit down where nobody could see me and rest for a couple of minutes. I dropped down into the heap and just then a thought struck me. I stood, stripped off my clothes. Quickly I sorted through the heap of uniforms, looking for a jacket and trousers my size. A lot of the stuff was worn and dirty, and some had holes the size of bullets—it was kind of sad seeing holes in the breast of a jacket and no hole in the back. But I found a pair of trousers that weren't too dirty, and a jacket with just a little tear in the sleeve. Finding a cap was easier, and two minutes later I was turned into a bluecoat.

I skipped on out from behind the heap of uniforms, grabbed a powder keg, hauled it out to the back of the wagon, and heaved it in. Cush was up in the front. He took a quick look back. "Hey, soldier, this here our wagon," he said.

I grinned. "Sure is, soldier."

Cush's mouth opened up, and he scrambled back over the kegs to me. "What the devil you do to yourself, Reb?"

"I joined up," I said, grinning some more.

Cush hopped out of the wagon. "Ain't you got a ounce of sense in your head, Reb? Captain Bartlett see you in that there blue jacket, he take you for a spy for sure."

"Spy? I'm not trying to spy."

"You explain that to Captain Bartlett. Reb, they shoot you if they think you spying. Now you git outten them there togs and git back into them old clothes of yourn."

Well, I felt like a fool, all right. It seemed like such a good idea—dress myself up like a Union fella, and maybe be able to sneak off out of there somehow. But I could see Cush was right. Captain Bartlett was bound to realize I was up to something. That was me—jump into things feet first and think about it later. Cussing myself for an idiot, I ran back into the warehouse and over to the mountain of clothes. Two colored privates were working over it, sorting out trousers, jackets, shirts, caps, into different heaps. I dashed around behind the pile. My old clothes were gone. I went back around to where the two privates were working. "You fellas see any old trousers laying around back there?"

"Ain't seen *nothin'* but old trousers," one of them said. "Mostly with the seat shot out of um." They both laughed.

"No, not uniforms, regular clothes."

"What you see back there is what is."

I raced around to the back of the pile again, and began digging through it, flinging clothes every which way. But my old clothes were gone. In the five minutes I'd been outside somebody'd come along and got rid of them.

"Blame it," I said. I ran back outside. The teamster soldiers were mounting up, climbing into wagons or onto lead horses. Somewhere a whistle blew. I ran up. "My clothes are gone, Cush."

"We got real trouble, Reb. You gotta get out of them things."

"I can't ride up to the front naked."

The whistle blew again. I swung up onto Regis, snapped the reins, and the next moment we were rolling on out of there, up the hill away from the docks and on toward the battlefront.

I'd put my foot in it again. How was I going to get out of that blame Yankee uniform? I wished there was some way I could turn myself black, for I'd be a whole lot less noticeable amongst those colored troops. All of a sudden it came over me what a funny thing that was to wish. I would have laughed out loud if it wasn't so worrisome—a white boy wishing he was a darky. But it was so. I'd have been a sight safer if I was colored right then.

Was there anything around I could paint myself up with? By now the air was full of red dust kicked up by the wagon wheels. I decided not to wipe it off when it fell on my face, but let it stick to the sweat. It wouldn't turn me black, but I'd seem sort of reddish brown if you didn't look too close. It'd help some.

By now we had got out of City Point and were getting into the countryside. I could hear in the distance the faint rumble of cannons, like thunder over the horizon. I turned my head back to Cush. "Are they fighting up there now?"

"There's shooting pretty near all the time at Petersburg, except at night, and sometimes then, too. The Rebs got theyselves dug in pretty good. Breastworks five feet high, with trenches behind and bombproof shelters dug in the dirt ten feet deep. You get yourself set up like that, a hundred men can hold off a thousand. We can't break through them, but they can't get outten there, neither."

He'd sort of forgotten I was a Reb, what

with me being in a blue uniform. "It seems like the Rebs can't be beat, then."

"Oh, we'll beat 'em. They starving in there right now. You won't see no pigeons anywheres in Petersburg, nor cats, nor dogs, and from what I heard the rats is disappearin' pretty quick, too."

I didn't want to believe that. "How come you know what's going on in there if the Federals can't get in?"

"Oh, they's no shortage of Rebs coming out and giving up. They say they wouldn't quit, but they's nothin' to eat but a pint of corn a day and a piece of bacon big enough to grease your plate with. They say they're beat and there ain't no use getting killed now."

I didn't like the idea of Southern soldiers giving up. "It must be only a few of 'em. I reckon most of 'em are full of fight."

"Oh, there's fight in 'em still. You see when we get there."

The thunder was louder, and now we could hear the pop-pop-pop of rifle fire. Ahead the wagon road rose up into low hills, winding along through what would have been cornfields if anybody was able to plant them. There wasn't much sign of fighting yet, except for a hole in the ground here and there where a shell landed. But there wasn't a tree anywhere in sight—not one. Just stumps: here a field of stumps where there'd been a woodlot, there another field of 'em. The Union troops had cut them all for firewood and timber to build huts and breastworks with.

We rolled on. Then we saw coming down the bare hill in front of us about a hundred men, walking slowly, their shoulders sagging. Guarding them were a dozen soldiers in blue, bayonets fixed. Cush pointed. "See what I told you? Reb prisoners. Taking them back to City Point to be shipped north."

I stared hard. A lot of them were wearing ordinary farmers' clothes, but there were enough gray uniforms mixed in so there wasn't a doubt about which side they were on. "Well, I bet we took a lot of your fellas, too."

Cush gave me a look. "You better watch how you talk so long as you got that blue uniform on."

"Nobody could hear me," I said.

"You want to git yourself hung, it's okay with me, but I'd just as lief skip it myself."

The Confederate prisoners were now

passing us. They looked bad—scrawny, so their uniforms hung on them loose, and a lot of them blotchy and red-eyed, like they were sick. I wished I could do something to cheer them up. I wished I had some food to give them, even a cool drink of cider. I wished I could just say something to them.

Then suddenly, in the middle of my wishing, there came a long whistle in the air. The prisoners and guards all threw themselves flat on the ground. Cush flopped off the seat and slid under the wagon. I sat there on Regis, frozen. There came a tremendous bang, like a clap of thunder right overhead, and something tore through the canvas wagon cover with a ripping sound. Back down the wagon train somebody shrieked, "I'm hit." There was a babble of voices. The men on the ground began slowly to stand up. Behind me whoever had got hit was shouting, "Oh, oh, oh."

I went on sitting where I was, still frozen. Cush slid out from under the wagon, and looked at me sitting there. "You better learn to move yourself a mite faster, Johnny Reb. You ain't going to last very long at the front lessen you do."

It was a lesson for me, all right. I knew about shells, but never had experience with them before. I'd know better next time. "Was it a big one?"

"Mortar, most likely. We're less than a mile from the lines up here. The Rebs can see the dust kicked up by the wagon train. Better when it's raining, for the dust don't rise."

The wagon train moved off. I was plenty nervous all right—my heart thumping away to beat the band, the sweat standing out on my forehead. I remembered what Pa said— there wasn't a man going into battle who wasn't scared. But I was powerful curious, too.

We rolled on up a hill. Along the crest a Union breastwork about five feet high ran in both directions as far as I could see. Here and there along the breastworks cannons poked their noses out toward Petersburg. A half dozen soldiers clustered around each cannon, and between them Federals leaned on the breastworks, their rifles resting on top of it. None of them was firing right then—just taking it easy.

The wagon train swung along behind the breastworks, about fifty yards back. The colored soldiers leapt out of the wagons and began unloading as quick as they could, hoping to get out of there before they got shelled.

Cush jumped out of the wagon, scooted around back, and began heaving a barrel out. I slid off Regis and went back there to help.

"You just keep out of sight, Johnny Reb." He hoisted the barrel onto his shoulder, and went off toward the breastworks.

I ought to stay out of sight; I knew that. But I was powerful curious to get a look at the battlefield. I clambered back to the front of the wagon and stood up on the seat. Now I could see beyond the breastworks. The hill fell away, the ground dropping off into a shallow valley. Then it rose up, and on top of the next hill, not a hundred yards away, was the Confederate breastworks. And in between, lying on both slopes of the hill, and down in the valley as well, were bodies—in gray uniforms —hundreds of them. Down at the bottom of the valley was a pit that had just been dug. A dozen Rebel soldiers were collecting the bodies, two men picking each one up by the arms and legs, and flinging them into that pit. Or, if the body didn't have arms and legs, just dragging it along by the shirt front. The Union soldiers up at the breastworks by me weren't paying attention to them. I figured it was allowed to go out and bury your dead.

It was clear enough what happened: the Confederate troops had come out of their lines, charged down their hill and up the other side, and had got all shot to pieces in the attack. My throat was dry and I swallowed hard. I just couldn't believe that all those men died together like that in one fell swoop, hundreds of them. One minute they were alive and the next minute they weren't; and now they were all being heaved into a pit. Those lives they were living, with all their feelings—being hungry, laughing at a joke, crying over someone dead, having a toothache, so much going on in each life—didn't mean anything at all. And the whole thing was a waste, for the attack hadn't got them anything.

Then I heard a sharp snap in the air and a ball flew by me. I saw Cush running back toward me. I jumped down from the wagon seat, onto the ground, and ran around to the back of the wagon. The main thing was to get the mules out of there soon as possible. Cush came up. "I'll help," I said.

"You dassn't."

"I'll stay by the wagon and unload for you. If anybody comes I'll jump inside like I was pushing the barrels along." Quickly I crouched down, scooped up a handful of dust, and closing my eyes, rubbed it onto my face. Then I stood, grabbed hold of the barrel Cush was wrestling with, and helped him heave it out of there.

"You don't look no more like a nigger than the mules does," Cush said.

"Careful how you talk about my mules, Yank."

So we went to work. And we'd got the wagon near cleaned out when I saw Captain Bartlett come riding a horse down the line towards us. My heart jumped. I knelt down behind Cush where I figured the captain couldn't see me and flung another handful of dust on my face.

Captain Bartlett rode by, about ten yards behind us. "Get moving, boys," he shouted. "Soon as you're empty move on out down the road." He went on down the line.

I stood up. "Come on, Cush, let's get them last two barrels out." We heaved one out, and Cush carried it off. I rested for a minute, and then here came Captain Bartlett back the other way toward me, shouting at the men as he went along. I swung myself up into the wagon and knelt down with my back to the tailgate, like I was tying my shoe. I couldn't see Captain Bartlett, but I could hear him shouting, "Keep moving, boys, keep moving." Then the horse clattered up behind my wagon and stopped. The light coming over my shoulder grew darker. "What have you got left in there, soldier?"

I didn't turn around. "Just that one barrel, sir. I'll get it out as soon as I get this mischievous shoe tied."

"Forget about the shoe, soldier. You want a bomb landing in here while you're tying your shoe?"

"Yes, sir." I straightened up and began sliding backward toward him, wrestling the barrel along.

"Blast it, soldier, you can't do anything that way. Hop on out of there."

Suddenly I heard Cush's voice. "I'll help him, Captain."

"Soldier, I said hop out of there."

I didn't have any choice. I slid backward over the tailgate onto the ground, one arm wiping at my face. Cush leaned in beside me and together we heaved the barrel out of there. Captain Bartlett sat on his horse, watching. Suddenly he shouted, "What's this? Who are you? You're not in my company." He looked closer. "Why you're white."

"No, sir, just awful light."

He stared at me a couple of seconds more. "Don't tell me that. You're not colored and you're not in my company. Turner, where did he come from?"

"He hurt his leg and asked for a ride up to the front."

Captain Bartlett didn't pay that any attention. "I know who you are," he said. "You're that Rebel boy." He leaned down from the horse and grabbed the front of my jacket. "Where'd you get this uniform? What are you doing in a Union uniform?" He shook me, rattling my bones. "Spying? Answer me. Where'd you get that jacket? Turner, did you give him this jacket?"

There was a bang up the line of wagons, a scream and a shout. Captain Bartlett swiveled the horse around. "I'll deal with you later." And he galloped off toward where the shell hit.

I looked at Cush. "What's going to happen?"

His eyes were wide and he looked scared. "Shoot you for a spy. You ought to of known better'n to put on a Federal uniform. Shoot me, too, for helping you, like as not."

Chapter Eleven

By now the Confederate shells were coming
down on us pretty hot, screaming overhead
and going off with a bang up or down the
line, or out on the wagon road we came up an
hour before. It was dreadful scary. What a
joke it would be if I was killed by my own
side. The colored troops were scrambling onto
the wagons and pulling out of there as quick
as they could. A couple of officers had gone
back down the wagon road a ways and were
waving their arms over their heads to speed
things up, although from the way the wagon

drivers were whipping their teams, it didn't look like they needed any reminding.

"Cush, what're we going to do?"

"You better make a run for it, Johnny Reb. You ain't got a chance otherwise."

"What about the mules?"

"Damn the mules. The best thing can happen to you, is get sent off to prison for twenty years. Them mules be long dead by the time you see 'em again."

"What about you?" I said.

"Maybe I can talk my way around it. I dassn't run. That's desertion and they shoot me for sure for that."

Blame me for an idiot. Why the devil did I ever put on that damn Yankee jacket? "It's all my fault, Cush."

"I'll talk them around, Johnny." But I could tell by the look on his face he was plenty worried. "You better run for it, else we both get blown up together." He turned and started to run off down the road after the wagon train. The minute he did there came a tremendous scream like a steam whistle straight over us. I threw myself down and so did he, and as we hit the ground there was a almighty roar all around us. I felt myself bounce off the ground, and for a minute I didn't know where I was. Then I realized I was lying there with half an inch of dirt all over me. I raised my head a little. Cush was lying flat on his back, dead still. The canvas cover to the wagon was ripped to pieces and the mules were whinnying and stamping around in their harness.

I turned my head to look down the road. The empty wagons were streaming off as fast as they could go, the drivers cussing out their teams and whacking at them with whips. And coming up the hill toward us was Captain Bartlett, riding hard. When he was about fifty yards away, he suddenly reined up. For a minute he sat on his horse staring at us lying flat on the ground with the tattered wagon behind us. Then he wheeled his horse around and started off after the wagon train. I lay still until he was out of sight. Then I got up on my hands and knees and crawled over to Cush. His eyes were closed and he was breathing fast, but he was alive. I grabbed his shoulder and shook him. He licked his lips but he didn't come around. I kneeled up so I could look him over. His cap was knocked off, and a little blood was oozing through the hair on top of his head. It didn't look too bad, but I didn't know anything about wounds. Maybe he was dying.

Then I noticed that his pants were torn at his left thigh and there was blood there, too. I held the tear in his pants open with my fingers. That wound didn't look too bad, neither. It didn't worry me so much as the head wound, because you could get your brains all scrambled by a hit without much showing. I knew, because I'd seen the body of a man who'd got kicked in the head when he was shoeing a horse. There wasn't hardly anything you could see except a little bump on his noggin, but he never woke up after he got kicked and died the next day.

It made me feel awful that Cush might die like that too, just go on lying there knowing nothing about it and die. I shook him again. "Cush, wake up." He licked his lips, but he didn't open his eyes.

It seemed like hours since that bomb went off on top of us, but it wasn't more than a couple of minutes. I looked down the wagon road again. The wagon train was about out of sight: all I could see was a cloud of dust hanging over the road. The shelling had eased up, but the bombs were still coming in. I stood up and ran back, crouching, to the mules. Up by the breastworks the soldiers were lying flat, waiting out the barrage. "Easy, Bridget," I said. "We're going this very minute." I jumped around to Regis and hopped on. But blame me if I could snap the reins to get the mules going. I sat there looking at Cush lying flat on his back in the road. I told myself he was a Yankee and a darky, and deserved what he got for coming down into our country to cause us trouble. Why should I save him? But suppose a shell landed on him? I couldn't let him die like that, lying in the dirt all alone. I just couldn't do it. We'd got to be friends by mistake.

I jumped off Regis, ran over to him, and shook him. "Cush, wake up." But he didn't open his eyes. I looked up, trying to think what to do. There, galloping up the wagon road, came three horsemen. I couldn't see who they were, but I wasn't about to take a chance. I had to get Cush out of there. I grabbed him by the shoulders, dragged him over to the wagon, and grunting and cussing, heaved him in. Then I raced around to the front, leapt on Regis, gave Bridget a crack with the whip to let her know it was urgent, and off we went, tearing at a near gallop along behind the Union breastworks, heading south. I didn't know what was out there, but it was the opposite direction from where the wagon train went, and that was good enough for me.

We came to another wagon track leading away from the breastworks down a hill. I took a glance back. In the distance I could see the three horsemen stopped about where me and Cush had got knocked over by the shell blast. I hit the mules a lick, and we tore down the hill. In a minute we were over the brow and out of sight.

Where the ground leveled off at the bottom, there were open fields rolling up and down low hills. Now that it was April, there was a touch of green in the fields where weeds and grass were beginning to grow, and here and there in the hills a few farmhouses and barns. There wasn't much else; there'd been fighting in these parts for a year now, since the siege of Petersburg started and everybody who could get out was gone. I pushed the mules on at a steady trot, following the road as it wound into the hills. The sound of shelling was dying out, and about twenty minutes later I'd put two or three miles between us and the front and felt a little easier. I took a look back at Cush, which wasn't hard, for the wagon cover was ripped to shreds. He was still lying where I'd heaved him in, but his eyes were open. "I notice you aren't dead," I said.

He sat up. "Mighty near. I got the worst blame headache you could think of."

"I'm mighty glad. For a while I was sure you was dying."

"I'm mighty glad myself," he said.

"I figured you didn't have a chance. But I flung you aboard anyway, just in case."

He reached down his leg and had a look at the cut. "That was mighty good of you, Johnny. The way them shells was coming in, by this time I likely be scattered across a half acre of ground."

"How's your leg feel?"

"The leg don't feel too bad. It's my blame head—it feels like they's something inside try-ing to hammer its way out."

"Listen, Cush. Just when I was leaving, three fellas on horseback came up and looked around where we got hit. Do you reckon it was Bartlett?"

"Can't tell. But it's mighty sure that somebody will be looking for us. They got you figured for a spy, and got me mixed up in it somehow. When Bartlett can't find hide nor hair of me, he'll start wondering, am I dead or did I run off with you?"

"Maybe I should have left you there."

"Maybe. But in the meantime I could of got blowed up."

I took a look around. Down the road a little there was a farmhouse set on one side of the road and a barn on the other. There was a hole in the roof of the house, but the barn looked solid. "What about holing up in that barn for a while, just to see if anyone's after us?" I said.

"What if they take a look inside?"

"I think we got to chance it," I said. "We can't stay out here in plain sight. No telling when they might come along."

So we did. The barn was standing wide open, like the farmer had got out of there so fast with his wagon and livestock he didn't take the time to close the door behind him. We drove the mules and the wagon inside and pulled the doors tight. It was pretty dark, but there were a couple of windows high up that gave some light. Besides, it was an old barn; the boards were shrunk, so there were a good many cracks between them where slices of light shone through.

I helped Cush out of the wagon, ripped some of the torn canvas from the wagon, and bandaged up his leg as good as I could. We sat there in the dark watching bits of dust float around in the slices of sun falling through the cracks, and in a little while we heard the sound of horses' hooves in the hard dirt road, coming fast. I jumped up and ran to the front of the barn, and Cush hobbled over after me. We stood side by side peeking out through the gaps in the boards. A half minute later three bluecoats tore by—a white officer and two colored soldiers.

"That's him, all right," Cush said.

"Who're the others?"

"One of 'em was Sergeant Crawford. I didn't see the other one good enough."

"What's he like, Sergeant Crawford?"

"Mighty tough. Been wounded three times and won't quit. Don't pay to mess with Sergeant Crawford."

We stood there for a minute thinking, and then Cush hobbled away from the barn wall and sat down again on the dirt floor. "First thing, we got to get ourselves outten these here blue jackets and into regular duds."

"How do you aim to do that?"

"Easiest way is to take 'em offen dead bodies. Ain't much shortage of that. These here Rebels, half of 'em don't have regular uniforms, but dressed like plain farmers."

"Aren't you afraid you'll get haunted afterward?"

"Naw. Everybody done it. Done worse— some soldiers go out at night after a battle and rob the bodies. You can find all kinds of truck on them bodies—money, gold rings, gold lockets with their sweethearts' pictures in 'em. Wouldn't do that myself. There's where you'd get in trouble with the spirits—cuttin' off some pore body's finger to get his ring."

"Would they do that?"

"Sure, if they can't get it off no other way."

Well, it might come down to robbing clothes off a body, but I wasn't in a hurry for it. But Cush was right, that we had to get out of the Union uniforms; Federals who came

181

across us would take me for a spy and him for a deserter. And if we were to run into Southern troops, they'd jail me and like as not shoot Cush where he stood. "Maybe we'll come across an empty house where they left some clothes," I said.

"Doubt it. By now the country around here is picked clean."

"Well, for now we got to chance it. We got to get out of this barn before Bartlett and them come back searching."

Cush shook his head. "Mostly likely won't come back. More'n likely they swing around on some other road where we might a gone."

"I don't know," I said. "It's a risk either way." To tell the truth, I had another reason for not sitting around that barn for hours; I was afraid Cush'd bring up that blame speech of Lincoln's. "If we get out of this, Cush, where do you aim to go?"

"I don't know. Sure like to get home to see how my mammy is doing. Ain't seen her for near a year. No telling what could have happened. I like to see if she all right."

"Mightn't they come looking for you back there?"

He picked up a little piece of straw that was lying on the dirt floor of the barn and stuck it in his teeth. "I reckon the Rebs is about beat. That's what they all say. They ain't gonna trouble theyselves about one little colored boy. All they know, I might have crawled off somewhere and died."

"What about your old master? What's he going to say when you turn up? Maybe he'll report you."

"Ain't likely he report me to the Yanks. That ain't the worrisome thing. Big problem is, how is things gonna be after the war? Lincoln promised that colored folk is free, but he ain't gonna be in the Shenandoah Valley seeing that it's so."

"You keep forgetting I'm a Reb."

"That's so, Johnny. It's on account of you being in that there blue jacket."

But I knew it wasn't. It was because he couldn't think of me as the enemy anymore. "Suppose the South wins after all? Suppose Lee schemes something out?"

"Lee's schemin' days is about over, I reckon. There ain't no chance the Rebs can win."

"There's always a chance," I said.

"And keep all us niggers slaves."

"Blame it all, Cush, don't jump so fast. Pa said the war didn't have nothing to do with slavery. He said most people'd be better off without them. We aren't for slavery." But the truth of it was, I wasn't sure anymore. If the war wasn't about slavery, what was it about? States' rights, sure—I didn't want the Yankees pushing us around any more than anybody did. But states' rights to do *what*? The whole thing had me mighty confused. I sure didn't want to see Cush going back to his old master and get whipped whenever the master felt like it, for I could see he wouldn't like getting whipped any more'n I did. And if it wasn't right for Cush to be whipped regular, why was it right for any of them to get whipped? "Well, we can't settle it right here. What we got to do is get ourselves safe somewhere. I reckon we ought to head off south. Bartlett and them can't follow us too far into Southern territory."

Cush shook his head mighty firm. "You can go south if you want, Johnny. I can't. Minute some cracker down there lays half a eye on me, I'm back in the slave cabins and due to stay there until the Federals get me out." He gave me a kind of funny look out of the sides of his eyes. "You best leave me here and get yourself someplace safe till you can get home to your ma."

Well, it was what Pa would want me to do, all right—not to trouble myself about some darky bluecoat, but get on home as quick as I could to take care of Ma and the little ones. "Cush, if I had any brains at all, that's exactly what I'd do. But seeing as I haven't got the sense I was born with, I reckon I better cart you along in the wagon until your leg gets healed up some."

He looked down at the ground, and patted a bit of dirt smooth. "I figured you say that, Johnny. I just wasn't sure."

Chapter Twelve

The best idea, we figured, was to head due west. This would carry us away from Petersburg and the fighting. Then when we'd got shet of the armies, we'd swing north and over the mountains into the Shenandoah Valley. Meanwhile, we'd keep our eyes out for ordinary farmers' clothes. Once we were dressed like plain folks, instead of soldiers, we'd be pretty safe, especially if Cush set up on the mule and I rode in the wagon. That'd seem natural enough to anybody from Virginia.

But until we could change our clothes,

we had to travel by night and hole up by day. We went along like that for three or four days, spending the days in empty barns or patches of woods away from the roads. Cush's leg got a little better each day, but he was still limping.

We were hungry a good deal of the time, but we were able to scrape up enough food to keep us going by rummaging around in empty barns and houses. There wasn't a whole lot left lying around, for people generally took what they had when they ran. But once we found a barrel of dried apples somebody had forgot; we put the whole thing in the wagon. Another time we came across a root cellar dug into the side of a hill where we found some potatoes and a chunk of cheese. Our best luck was to run into a chicken wandering loose in a barnyard. We caught it, wrung its neck, plucked it and then cleaned it with Cush's bayonet, and cooked it over a fire we made in the barn. That was the best-tasting chicken I ever ate.

If we hadn't the mules and the wagon, we could have cut across country. With the wagon, we had to stick to the roads, and we were always going by farmhouses where they hadn't run off but could see us going by in the moonlight if they took the trouble to look out the window. We skirted around any towns we came to as best we could, but we weren't always able to do it. We just kept on going, across Hatcher's Run, and White Oak Creek, and smack through a place called Blacks and Whites, which gave us the first laugh we got out of anything for a while. And then to a place called Dudley's Bridge, and Farmville, crossing railroad tracks and rivers all the way —the Sandy River, the Bush River, the Buffalo River. Finally we came to the Appomattox River and began to follow that along, for I knew that it went generally west.

What bothered us most was that we couldn't get shet of the war. We figured by now we'd left it behind us; but we hadn't, for the whole time we were traveling we could hear to the north of us the steady thunder of cannons. Sometimes at night we could see the sky there lit up with flashes from the shells. It seemed like the war was traveling along with us a few miles away. So we couldn't turn north toward the Shenandoah, but had to keep traveling west.

A couple of times we talked about turning north toward the fighting, where there was bound to be bodies we could strip for clothes. But we dassn't: with the mules we'd get spotted a mile away. So on we went, and we were so busy hunting up food and keeping out of the way of the war that it wasn't until the third day, when we were holed up in a nice thick patch of woods by a stream, that Cush brought up that cussed speech of Lincoln's. "Now's the chance," he said. "We ain't got nothin' better to do except listen to them cannons firing."

Well, I knew it had to come sooner or later. I got hot. "I'm too blame hungry to think about it, Cush."

"It take your mind offen your belly," he said. He reached into the breast pocket of his blue jacket and took out that little scrap of paper. It was so smudged and worn I couldn't hardly read it, but by this time I'd got it near memorized. I reckoned I was the only person in the entire Confederacy who learnt a speech of Abe Lincoln's by heart.

"I was thinking of taking a little snooze," I said.

"Now don't try to get out of it. You promised." He handed me the scrap of paper and moved over close so's he could read along with me.

I was pretty well stuck. Why in tarnation had I decided to learn Cush wrong? Well, I guess I could remember why. It made sense at the time—it seemed like the right thing to do. Same as deciding to join up with the wagon train, and going back on my promise to Pa. It went to show that a lot of times what seems right at the time doesn't turn out right. I hoped the whole thing would learn me a lesson. I didn't know if it would, but I hoped so, for I didn't want to get into any more pickles like this one.

I took the piece of paper and looked at it. "Cush, I got an idea we ought to start all over again. My head's so confused by everything the last few days I forgot what half of this here thing says."

"I didn't forget it," he said. "Four score and seven years ago, our fort fighters broke—"

"Well I'll be blowed, Cush," I said, feeling hot and sweaty. "Is that the way I learned it to you?"

"Sure it is."

"There. Just goes to show how addled

up my mind is. It isn't that at all. It's 'Four score and seven years ago, our forefathers brought—' "

"You mean you learned me that part wrong?" He gave me a steady look.

"It seems like I did. That part, anyway."

"What about this here?" He jabbed his finger down onto the paper. "Where it says 'a new nation, conceived in libraries.' "

I couldn't look at him. "Blamed if I know how I got so addled up. It's supposed to say, 'conceived in liberty.' "

"You mean you been learning this whole speech wrong?" He stared at me pretty wild.

I put on a puzzled look, like I couldn't figure out how it happened. "Seems like I did. I don't understand it."

He jabbed his finger at the paper again. "What about this here part, where it says, 'Brought forth on this comet a new nation dedicated to the proposition that all men are created eagles?' "

I looked down at the ground. "That ain't right, neither," I whispered.

"What's it supposed to be, Reb?" he said, mighty fierce.

I went on looking at the ground. "It's supposed to say 'All men are created equal.' "

He didn't say anything, and the time ticked along, with only the babbling of the stream and a little breeze in the trees making the only sound. Then he said, "You been learning me the whole thing wrong."

I looked up at him. "I guess I was just so worried about Ma and the little ones back home my mind got tangled up." I looked him in the eye as best as I could.

He stared at me hard. "You wasn't tangled up. You done it on purpose."

"Honest, Cush, I didn't."

"Yes, you did, Johnny. You done it on purpose, for you was determined to keep me from finding out the real meaning of it—about all men being created equal—about what Lincoln promised, what the Declaration promised. You ain't no different from the rest of the buckra."

"That isn't true," I said. It wasn't neither, for I was only trying to get out of learning him to read.

"God damn you, Johnny. I trusted you was learning me right."

I was beginning to lose my temper myself. "You got to blame yourself, Cush. You captured me and was sitting up there high and mighty, waving my great-grampa's sword around like you were King of the Moabites. Why should I learn you right?"

He snatched the speech out of my hand and stood up. "I don't trust you no more, Johnny. I ain't staying here one more second."

I jumped up. "Go on then. You'll only get yourself killed for it, and serve you right, too."

He turned and started off through the patch of woods, limping pretty bad. My heart was sick, watching him. He couldn't begin to run. The minute anyone saw him, he was a gone goose. Some farmer was bound to see him and fetch some Confederate troops. He didn't have a chance of getting away at all.

"Damn you, Cush," I shouted. He was out of sight in the trees and I didn't know if he heard me. I started after him. Even with his limp he was making pretty good time, for I didn't spot him until I came to the edge of the woods. He was about fifty yards into a field, heading toward a little farm road at the other side. He was cutting across it at an angle, so he couldn't see what was coming along the farm road behind him, but I could. "Cush," I screamed.

He stopped in the middle of the field and turned halfway around to look at me. "Come back, Cush," I screamed. I pointed back up the farm road. About a dozen Confederate cavalrymen were sailing down the road, pulling a cloud of dust along behind them. Cush took one look and began to hobble back toward me across the field as fast as he could. Curse that speech, I thought. Curse everything.

He was almost at the woods before they spotted him in that blue jacket. Then two of them wheeled their horses off the road and started for us. I raced back to where the mules were hid, ripping off my blue jacket as I went. I flung it off in among the trees. Cush came hobbling along after me, and right behind him there came the two cavalrymen, waving their revolvers. "Wait," one of them shouted.

We raised our hands over our heads. "Don't shoot," I shouted. "We aren't Federals."

They rode up to us. "What do you mean you aren't Federals?"

"Honest," I said. "I scooped that jacket off a body."

He cocked his head. "That your nigger?"

"He's ours," I said. "Pa got killed at Cedar Creek, and him and me was in a wagon train going to Richmond with beef and sech, and the Sheridans got us and killed a lot of Mosbys that was with us. We been on the run ever since, trying to get home."

"Where's home?"

"Shenandoah. Halfway up High Top Mountain."

"You say your Pa was killed at Cedar Creek?" the cavalryman said.

"He got hit there. He came home and died."

"What was his outfit?"

"Company K, Tenth Virginia Volunteers," I said.

He turned and looked at the other cavalryman. "That right? Were they there?"

"I think that's right," the other one said. "They were with Early, anyway. It's likely they were at Cedar Creek."

The first one shook his head. "I don't buy it. Who'd be so stupid as to dress up a nigger in a Federal jacket?"

"His clothes was plumb falling off him," I said. "I didn't want to haul a naked nigger around where anybody'd see him. So I scooped some stuff off some corpses."

"You haven't got much brains, son, but you got more brains than that."

"Leave them go," the other one said. "We got to make Appomattox before nightfall."

"I don't trust it," the first one said.

"Well, all right," the other one said. "Take the nigger if you want. But we can't be hauling this boy and his wagon along with us. Slow us down too much, getting into Appomattox. The Federals are right on our tails as it is."

So the first one hauled Cush up behind him on the horse, and off they went through the woods. I ran after them to the edge of the woods and stood there watching them gallop across the field and then disappear down the farm road in the cloud of dust.

Chapter Thirteen

I had my work cut out for me now, and I knew it. They'd take Cush into Appomattox and lock him up somewheres, I figured, unless they got tired of him and decided to shoot him along the way. I heard of Appomattox, for teamsters were always talking about places where they'd been, but I didn't know anything about it. Whatever it was, it did seem plain that there was going to be some fighting there. There'd be bodies, sure enough, and if I was smart enough I'd be able to get some clothes for us. Of course, that wasn't going to do Cush any good unless I could get him sprung loose from wherever they locked him up. But I figured there was a chance I could talk them into it if I cried and said Ma was sick and we just had to have our nigger back to keep the farm going. I could try, anyway.

I picked up the blue jacket out of the bushes where I'd flung it and threw it in the back of the wagon, just in case I ran into Federals. Then I drove the mules out of the woods, across the field, and onto the farm road toward Appomattox.

There was cannon firing pretty frequent, a whole lot closer than it had been before. It sounded like it wasn't more'n three or four miles up to the north. Sometimes I could even hear rifles pop-popping away. There was going to be bodies enough, if I could only find them.

I hadn't been going for more than a half hour when I heard the sounds of horses behind me, and some shouts. I swung the mules and the wagon off the road into the grass along the edge, jumped off Regis, ducked down behind the wagon, and took a look back down the road. Around a bend came a passel of cavalry, raising up a storm of dust. At first I couldn't tell whether they were Confederate or Union, but then they swept by me, and through the dust I saw the blue uniforms. There were at least a hundred of them, and they were going full tilt down the road toward Appomattox. Were they chasing the Confederate cavalrymen who had took Cush away? It seemed likely. Even if they weren't, the way they were galloping they'd bump into them soon enough. That was mighty worrisome, for if it came to a fight, Cush'd be in the middle of it.

I stood by the roadside, waiting until the dust settled, and watching to see if any more Federals were coming along. Then I got back on Regis and started off for Appomattox again. And it surprised me to come upon those bodies scattered along both sides of the road ahead of me, for I hadn't heard a sound of fighting—not a shout, not a shot, not galloping horses. There was a couple of horses down, too. I pulled the mules and the wagon up to the side of the road and climbed off Regis. For a bit I stood there, looking down the road at the bodies, feeling kind of sick to my stomach. But I had to do it, so I walked forward, easy, like I was afraid of taking them by surprise. As I got closer I saw that there were blue uniforms as well as gray. There'd be some plain farmers' clothes, too, I reckoned. I kept on going, wondering if any of 'em was still alive. Then I was amongst them—five or six of them on either side of the road, scattered every which way, like they'd been flung down by a giant hand from above. Some were on their backs with their arms out, some facedown—one had even died kneeling. They looked so human, but of course they weren't human anymore—no more human than dirt and stones. Some of 'em didn't look like they'd been touched—I couldn't see anything wrong with them. But others were pretty well messed up. One had been sliced across the stomach, so half his guts was spilled out onto the road. Another was missing part of his head—just one eye left. The blood was still wet on them.

I felt sick as could be. I didn't see how I was going to make myself undress any of them. I looked around. A little bit farther along I saw a fella wearing ordinary brown trousers and a brown shirt. I went over to him. He'd been shot in the side of the head. I knelt down over him and began unbuttoning his shirt as fast as I could move my hands. Then I raised him up, jerked the shirt off his arms, and dropped him. A minute later I had his pants off. I felt so sorry for him, lying half naked, I couldn't look at him, and went along a little farther looking for another one wearing ordinary clothes. And I hadn't got more than ten yards when I heard a little moan. I looked around, and saw a man propped up on a little rise of ground by the edge of the road. He was wearing regular clothes and had his arms folded over his chest. I knelt down by him. "Where were you hit?"

"In my lung here. You got any water? I'm dry as a bone."

"I'll get some. Where's your canteen?"

"Lost it. Maybe one of the other fellas has one."

"I got some in my wagon." I trotted back to it, got my water bottle, and brought it to the wounded man. He took a long drink, choked and spluttered and took another drink. "That's a help," he said.

"Where'd your outfit go?"

"All shot to pieces. The Yankees blew right through us."

"If I can find them I'll tell them where you are. Did they head for Appomattox?"

"I guess some of 'em will make it there."

"Was there a fella carrying a nigger in a Federal uniform with them?"

"There was," he said. "I don't know about now. It don't much matter. The whole thing's over. We ain't had nothing to eat for two days. The fellas was eating horse corn. Soaked it water to soften it up, but it still like to bust their teeth."

"Maybe General Lee will think of something."

"He can think all he wants. It's soldiers he needs and he ain't got 'em. A lot of them skedaddled for home when they seen how things was. I wished I did it myself. Damn shame to get it like this when it's almost over. Another day or two and I'd be safe out of it." Suddenly he moaned, and lay there biting his lip.

"Does it hurt real bad?"

"About as bad as can be. I'm a goner. Doubt if I last until nightfall."

That would be another set of regular clothes. But I couldn't do it—I just couldn't sit around there waiting for him to die, so as to strip the clothes off him. It was too much for me.

I hated to leave him there, but there wasn't anything I could do for him. So I gave him another drink of water and went back to the wagon. I stripped off the blue uniform, and climbed into the clothes I'd taken from the corpse. I didn't like it none, for there was the feeling of death on them, and it seemed like it might rub off on me. I flung the Federal uniform off to the side of the road and started up again, driving careful till I got past the bodies so as not to run any of 'em over. Once I was a ways down the road, I felt a whole lot better, for at least I'd got shet of that cursed uniform. I needed another set of clothes for Cush, but I didn't doubt there'd be bodies enough to go around. I just hoped that me and Cush weren't among them.

Where was Cush? Was he dead? Was he lying shot up somewhere? There was no way to be sure, but it was most likely they'd taken him to Appomattox. There wasn't anything better for me to do but head there, keep my eyes open, and hope for the best.

So that's what I did—just pushed the mules on down the road, watching for signposts. Signs of war were everywhere: a wagon tipped up on its side with a wheel off and a dead horse still tangled up in the harness; a house burnt to the ground, with the chimney standing up out of a heap of charcoal; rifles and knapsacks by the side of the road where they'd got dropped by soldiers too tired and sick to care anymore and had skipped off for home. Here and there I came across stragglers, sitting by the side of the road, or walking along toward me, trying to get themselves out of the war. And always the sound of cannons thundering. On I went, passing through little farm villages, and then I began to see signs for Appomattox Court House. Even with a name like that, it figured to be little more than a farm village. I came around a bend, and through a cluster of trees down the road I saw the steeple of a little church and the roof of a good-sized building I figured had to be the courthouse.

I reined up the mules and sat looking around. It was getting on toward nightfall. On down the road I could see a bunch of Confederate soldiers sitting by the side of the road, resting. All around me there was the sounds of war in every which direction—the thunder of cannons, the faint popping of rifles, over there some horses trotting, over here closer by somebody shouting orders. It seemed like I was smack dab in the middle of the thing.

I was scared to be going among people, instead of hiding out the way we did the past few days, but I had to find Cush. So I got the mules started again and went along down the road until I came abreast of the soldiers resting by the road. They looked mighty tired: a lot of them were lying flat on their backs. I stopped the mules. "Any of you fellas seen some cavalry come through here with a nigger in tow—a nigger wearing a Federal jacket?"

"Nigger's making theirselves pretty scarce around here along about now."

That was worrisome. "You think they'll be fighting right here in Appomattox?"

"Ain't any other place it can be. The only army Lee's got left is here."

"Is General Lee here?" It would be exciting to see him, for he was the greatest general in history. "Do you think I could get a look at him?"

"Look at him all you want, if you come acrost him."

"Did you ever see him?" I asked.

"Never did. 'Spect I may now, for if there's to be a fight here, he'll be in it."

This wasn't finding Cush. "Thanks," I said and flipped the lines to get the mules moving again. Now I could see the village pretty clear through the trees—the courthouse, a few houses here and there, a white church. Out in the fields along the road soldiers were camped everywhere, setting up tents, getting the fires going, a lot of them just sitting and resting. I kept an eye out for any kind of a place that looked like it might be a prison of some kind—a barn with a couple of guards in front of it, maybe just an old horse corral where they'd got prisoners fenced in. But I didn't see anything of the kind.

Then I came into town. Directly ahead of me was the courthouse—a big stone building. Some soldiers were lounging on the courthouse steps. Off to one side of it was a good-sized brown house with a porch along the front, set into a nice piece of lawn. Soldiers were standing around on the porch here, too. I pushed the mules along to the house and climbed down off Regis, glad to stand up for a spell. I walked across the lawn up to the porch to where the soldiers were lounging around the door. "I'm looking for a nigger wearing a Federal jacket who was took prisoner by mistake. He's our nigger. He isn't a Union soldier, he's just a plain nigger."

"I don't know about no niggers," one of 'em said. "But they got somebody locked up in a barn outside town somewheres."

There was just no way to guess—no way to know if Cush was dead or alive, no way to know if he was in Appomattox, no way to know anything about him at all. "Where exactly is this here barn?"

The soldier shrugged, but another one pointed off to the south. "Down that road a couple of miles."

It was the only hope. I climbed back on the mules and headed south down a road that passed under an alley of trees. Appomattox was in pretty good shape—a nice, quiet little town with purple lilac bushes blooming in people's dooryards, white blossoms drifting down from apple and pear trees behind the houses. It was a blame shame that soon enough it would be all shot up, houses burnt down, trees smashed, maybe even that court-house knocked to pieces. And a lot of bodies scattered around the fields, the front lawns, lying under the lilac bushes and the apple trees so that the blossoms drifted down on their faces. I hated to think of it.

By the time I found that barn, it was near dark. But they'd got a fire going close by that lit things up pretty good. A half dozen soldiers were standing around the fire, eating, or smoking pipes, and a couple more were walking guard duty around the barn.

I got off Regis and started for the barn. I was blame tired and hungry and wanted nothing more than to lie right down where I was and go to sleep. But I kept on putting one foot in front of the next until I came up to where the soldiers were standing around the fire. Now I could see that it was an old tobacco barn, with the slats set a few inches apart to allow the air to blow through and dry out the tobacco. There wouldn't be any problem seeing what they'd got inside if I could get close enough.

"You got any niggers in there?" I said.

They were eating hardtack — breaking off

chunks and taking them with a mouthful of water so they could chew it soft enough to swallow. A couple of them shrugged. "What's it to you?" one of them said.

"Our nigger was wearing a Federal jacket and got took prisoner by mistake."

"I shouldn't wonder," one of them said. "He's lucky he ain't shot."

"He's not a Federal soldier. He's just a plain nigger. Ma'll be mighty upset if we lose him. He's always been a good worker."

He shrugged again. "Go have a look."

I walked over to the barn. A tobacco barn like that generally had a big door at each end so you could drive a wagon in one side and out the other. The doors were closed, and a guard was leaning on the doors at one end. I slipped up to the side, and peered in through the cracks between the slats. It was pretty dark in there—just a little light filtering in from the campfires outside. "Cush," I said in a loud whisper. I heard a movement. "Cush."

"That you, Johnny? I don't believe it."

"It's me."

Suddenly he appeared out of the darkness and stood with his face by the slats, so the firelight flickered across it. There was a bruise on his cheek and blood around his ear. "What'd they do to you, Cush?"

"Slammed me around a little just to keep theyselves cheered up. How you find me here?"

"I asked around. What's going to happen?"

"They talking about shooting me. Don't know as they will or they won't."

"Blame it, Cush. I'll get you out."

Then the soldier guarding the door trotted over. "What're you doing here?"

"This here's our nigger. He isn't any Federal soldier. He was just wearing a Federal jacket."

"I don't care whose nigger he is. You ain't supposed to be talking to the prisoners. Now scat."

"Ma's going to be awful sad if we don't get him back."

"If I was you, I'd forget about that nigger and take yourself home. Some of the fellas around here just plain can't stand the sight of a nigger in a soldier suit, and if they ketch him alone they're likely to spit him like a roast chicken. Can't say I like it myself, but my job

is to guard him, and they won't get in while
I'm here."

"I just got to get him out. Ma needs him
on the farm real bad. He's the only one who
can handle our mules," I said, hoping he
didn't notice our mules out by the road.

He shook his head. "Ain't much chance
of gettin' him out, I reckon. Now you scat."

"I just got to talk to somebody about it."

He spit. "Go see Colonel Marshall then.
Now git."

"Where's he at?"

"Back in town somewheres." This time
he raised his rifle and stuck the bayonet about
six inches from my belly. "Now git."

I turned and trotted back across the field
to where the mules were standing, climbed
onto Regis, and headed back for town. I was
awful scared for Cush. It seemed like everybody was out to get him. I pushed the mules
on back to town. I figured the Confederate
headquarters were set up in that courthouse,
but when I got there, the soldiers who had
been lounging in front of it were gone. I
climbed up the steps and pulled on the door.
It was locked tight. I went back down the
steps and ran around to the side to get a look

at the windows. There were no lights in them, upstairs or down. So I climbed back on Regis and pushed on down to the house where I'd talked to the soldiers before, feeling just as weary as I could be. The soldiers were still on the porch of the house. I climbed off Regis and went up to them. "I'm looking for Colonel Marshall."

The soldier laughed. "He's asleep. He ain't hardly been off his horse for three days. He's plumb tuckered out. He said don't wake him up for nothing 'lessen the Yankees is coming in through the front door."

There wasn't any point in arguing, I could see that clear enough. I was just a kid, and Cush was of even less account than me, for he was black. "What time'll he get up?"

The soldier shrugged. "When he's ready. Not before daylight, I don't reckon."

So there it was. I was plumb tuckered out myself. The heart was pretty much gone out of me right then, and I figured I better get some sleep. In fact, there wasn't anything else I could do. So I pulled the wagon down the road a bit and off into a field where nobody was likely to pay any attention to me, unharnessed the mules, tethered them under a tree where they could graze, and lay down in the wagon.

For a moment I lay there wondering what Cush was thinking and feeling right then. Suddenly I realized I was hearing a sound I'd heard all my life—the spring peepers. They were singing away, chirping and peeping, just like they did back home. It near broke my heart to hear them, for it reminded me of the old days, before the war, when Sam and Sarah were babies in their cradles. Sometimes, when the evening was nice, me and Ma and Pa would sit on the front steps after supper, just resting. Pa'd smoke his pipe and him and Ma would talk, and I'd snuggle down between them, listening, feeling mighty comfortable with myself. There would be the sound of the peepers. At that time I didn't even know where the sound came from, or who was making it. It was just a pretty sound, and I liked it.

And here I was, in the middle of a terrible war, with two armies getting ready to pounce on each other, and it didn't matter to the peepers one ounce—not one ounce. I reckoned they figured that if human beings were so foolish as to kill one another by the

213

thousands—tons of corpses piled up every-where—worse luck to them. The peepers would go about their business all the same, chirping and peeping, no matter what human beings did. Thinking about this, I could feel the tears start up behind my eyes. But I was too tired even to cry, and I fell asleep.

Chapter Fourteen

I woke up when the sun started up over a line of trees to the east and fell into my eyes. I sat up in the wagon and rubbed my eyes. I felt a whole lot better, but just as hungry as I could be. I couldn't think when I'd been that hungry. Now I could see the sun sparkling off a little pond. I took the mules back there, watered them, splashed my face, and had a drink myself. I was starting back for the wagon when some cannons suddenly started to thunder off to the south, not too far away. They were fighting again.

All the more reason to get Cush out of there, in case the battle came our way. I harnessed up the mules as quick as I could and drove them back to the house where Colonel Marshall was.

The soldiers were gone. My heart sank. I'd missed him. I sat there on Regis, looking around. In fact, there was nobody in sight — no soldiers, no ordinary people, nobody. Off to the south the cannons were still pounding away. The fighting was still far enough away so I couldn't hear any rifle fire. Maybe there was a chance Lee would drive Grant off.

Then I noticed a plume of smoke rising up from the chimney of the house. Somebody was home after all. I climbed down off Regis and trotted around to the back of the house, for it figured to be a kitchen fire. The kitchen window was open about a foot, and coming out of it was the smell of bacon frying and coffee steaming in the pot. My mouth began to water, and I licked my lips. Oh, my, how good that smelled. I slipped up to the window and took a peek in. An old black woman was bent over the stove, stirring something — scrambled eggs, I figured.

It was more than I could stand. I darted away from the window and knocked on the back door. I could hear the woman thump across the kitchen, and then the door opened. "I'm looking for Colonel Marshall." I licked my lips.

"They all gone," she said. "Ain't nobody here but the Marse McLean."

Why hadn't I waked up earlier? "Do you know where they went?"

"I dunno nothing about it. Now you git. I got to fix Marse McLean his breakfast."

I licked my lips, but I wouldn't beg. "Maybe Marse McLean knows where they went."

"Now, I ain't gonna bother him with no foolishness. I got to git his breakfast." She started to close the door, but as she did it a man dressed in a suit and a stringtie came into the kitchen.

"Who is it, Aunt Sally?"

"Just a boy."

She opened the door a little so he could see me, and I stepped inside so she couldn't close it on me. "Sir, I'm looking for Colonel Marshall. They got our nigger locked up with the Federal prisoners in a tobacco barn, because he was wearing a Federal jacket I put on him."

"Colonel Marshall is gone. They left at daybreak. Lee is trying to break out through the Yankee lines to the south. You better clear out, son. They'll be fighting all around here."

"Sir, is there anyone else who could get our nigger out?" The smell of that ham and eggs blame near floored me, and I licked my lips.

He shook his head. "They're all gone. Lee sent everybody he could scrape together into the fight."

I licked my lips again—I couldn't help it. "Sir, maybe if you was to tell them soldiers to let him go—"

He shook his head. I licked my lips once more. He smiled. "Son, there's nothing I can do for your nigger. But you look like you wouldn't mind a little breakfast. Aunt Sally, give the boy my breakfast and cook up another for me."

"Marse McLean, if you gonna feed everybody who knocks on your kitchen door—"

He smiled again. "No, no, Sally, it's all right. There'll be enough inhumanity in Appomattox today without our adding to it. Eat hearty, son." He left.

The woman grumbled, but she filled up a tin pie plate with ham and eggs and a couple of biscuits and poured me a cup of coffee, and I sat down at the kitchen table and ate. Well, ate isn't the exact word; I shoveled that ham and eggs home so fast I was gasping for breath at the end and had to sit there blowing on my coffee until I could get myself calmed down enough to drink it.

It was the best meal I ate in two weeks, since I left home. The truth was, I felt so comfortable sitting there in that kitchen with all those good smells around me, I couldn't get myself out of that chair. I had to find Colonel Marshall—I knew that. But what did it matter if I sat there just five minutes longer? So I did, smelling the food, looking around at that warm, clean, sunny kitchen, and dreaming that I lived there and had nothing to do for the rest of morning but look forward to dinner.

Then suddenly I heard voices coming from the front room, and I was brought back to myself. I looked at the kitchen clock and saw a half hour had gone by. Suppose they shot Cush while I was sitting there? I jumped up. It sounded to me like the cannons were closer now. What was I going to do? Maybe the best thing was to go back to that barn and see what was happening there. Maybe Colonel Marshall had come back. Or some other officer was there. Or the soldiers guarding it had heard the fighting coming toward them and had run off. It could be anything. "Thank you," I said to the woman, and headed for the door.

Then into the kitchen came Mr. McLean with three or four Confederate officers behind him. "This is the kitchen," Mr. McLean said. He pointed out the back window. "There are stalls for four horses in the barn, but not much fodder, I'm afraid."

The officers stood at the kitchen door, looking around.

"I don't suppose General Lee will be very hungry, considering the circumstances," he went on, "but we'd like to show the Yankees some hospitality. I'll see what we can rustle up."

The officer nodded, and then they left the kitchen. Suddenly Mr. McLean noticed me standing by the door with my hand on the knob. "You better go along, son. There's some important visitors on their way here."

The cook was staring at Mr. McLean. "Marse McLean, did I hear right? Gin'ral Lee comin' to this house?"

He nodded. "He's going to meet with Grant here in about a half hour."

"Sir," I said, "does that mean the war's over?"

He shook his head. "Depends on whether they agree on terms. We can't be sure yet. Now you go along, son. I've got things to attend to."

"Does it mean we lost?"

"Nothing's settled yet, son. Now you go along."

So I said "thank you" to Mr. McLean in case I hadn't said it before, ran out the back door, and around front to the mules. All sorts of things were flying through my head. I'd be blame glad to have the war over, but it made me feel kind of sick inside to think that after everything, we were most likely going to lose. I wondered if Pa was up there looking down on us. How would he feel about getting killed for nothing?

But the war wasn't over yet. Off toward

the south somewhere cannons were banging away and rifles going pop-pop-pop. What was I going to do? It didn't seem like I had much choice: the only thing to do was get myself back out to that barn and see how things stood.

I started for the mules, and then it came to me that they'd be a sight safer right where they were, for it wasn't likely there was going to be any fighting where Lee and Grant were meeting. So I hauled the mules and wagon off into the field behind Mr. McLean's house, and then I set off at a run for that tobacco barn. It was a good piece of running. I began to sweat pretty quick, and by the time I was halfway there my breath was coming hard and my legs ached. But I kept at it, and then I rounded a bend and the tobacco barn came into sight, out in the middle of that field.

There was nobody there—nobody at all. The firing off to the south was a good deal closer now: I reckoned the battle wasn't more than a mile or so away. I figured the soldiers that were there by that barn the night before had gone off to fight. And where was Cush?

I started across the field to the barn, and then suddenly the barn door flung open, and out came two Confederate soldiers, with Cush between them. "Wait," I screamed. I began charging across that field as fast as I could run. "Wait."

The soldiers stopped and looked across the field at me. I came running up. "Don't shoot him," I shouted. "The war's over." I stood there panting. Cush's nose was bleeding and there was a scratch down the side of his neck. He didn't say anything—he knew he'd best keep quiet.

"The war's over?" one of the soldiers said. "Could of fooled me." He pointed off to the south where the guns was banging away. "Seems like they forgot to tell them fellas."

"It's really over," I shouted. "General Lee's meeting with Grant right back in town. They're settling it this very minute." I hoped that was so.

The two soldiers looked at me. "What makes you so all-fired sure?"

I calmed down a little. "It's true," I said. "Mr. McLean told me. I was at his house and some of Lee's officers came in and said they was going to meet there with Grant."

"McLean? Who's he?"

Was it really over? Could I stall these fellas off until it stopped? "Please. He's not a Federal. He's just a plain nigger. I put that jacket on him so as not to haul him around naked where people could see him."

"That wasn't real smart." He spit. "Where you from, boy?"

"Shenandoah. Pa got shot at Cedar Creek. We just got to have our nigger back to work the farm." Then I noticed something. Off toward the south the sound of shooting was dying down. "Listen," I said.

We all stood there, dead still. There were still some rifles popping away, but we couldn't hear any cannons banging. "I told you," I said. "It's over."

"Keep quiet so's I can hear."

Now the rifle fire was dying out, just a pop here and there. We stood listening. Then it was dead still. The only sound was a couple of robins out in the field singing "cheer-up" cheerily.

"What do you make of it?" one of the Confederate soldiers said.

"Something's up."

"I keep telling you," I said. "It's over."

"Boy, I told you to keep quiet." He squinted at the other soldier. "I don't trust it.

May be some kind of a trick. You can't tell with them Yankees. We ought to have kilt this nigger last night when we had the chance."

"Please," I said.

Nobody said anything for a minute. Then, from off in the distance, there came the sound of a bugle, a small sound, but clear. "It *must* be over," said one of the soldiers.

"Let's finish off this here Yankee nigger afore it's too late."

Then the bugle came again, closer this time, and right after it the sound of horses hooves thrumming on the dirt. We turned to look. Coming down the road was a troop of Union cavalrymen. They were raising a lot of dust, but I could see clear enough the Union flag coming along in front.

"Let's go," one of the soldiers said. They turned and ran. Cush dropped straight down onto his knees. "Thank the Lord," he said.

Me and Cush walked back to Appomattox, going slow on account of Cush's leg. Oh, my, the excitement there was something. There were soldiers everywhere, Union and Confederate, the blue and the gray, talking with one another. The Confederates were all scrawny and hungry, and some of the Federals were giving them whatever they had by way of food—hardtack, dried beef, coffee, and such. For us, there was a terrible sadness to it. But it was a relief, all the same. For now I'd go on home, and look after Ma and the little ones. I'd been gone for two weeks, and they'd be worrying over me now, and praying like as not. But I'd get the mules home safe, and then I'd keep my promise to Pa. Whatever happened to us from now on, it couldn't be as bad as it was the last terrible four years.

We got hold of a little dried beef and hardtack and went out into the field where I'd tethered the mules, and sat in the grass by the wagon, chewing the beef and talking. "You still aim on going home to see your mammy, Cush?"

"Got to," he said. "Got to see how things is going to be now. Mebbe I can go to school." He gave me a look out of the corner of his eyes. "Learn me to read from somebody who'll learn me right this time."

I blushed. "Blame it, Cush, how was I know we would be friends?"

"Kind of took me by surprise, too," he

said. "But I don't know if most white folks are gonna take to it."

"You can't tell, Cush." Then I said, "You fixing to ride in the wagon?"

"That there's the point. How do you think white folks'll take to that—seeing the colored boy in the wagon and the white boy riding the mule? You think they like it?"

I thought about it a little. "I don't know, Cush. Maybe. Maybe not. We got to wait and see."

"You think if you was to take me home, you mammy say, 'Come in and sit down, Cush. Help yourself to that there piece of chicken and them hot biscuits?' "

Well, I knew Ma. She'd be polite to Cush and give him some biscuits and gravy, but she'd bring it to him in the backyard, and he'd have to sit there on the woodpile and eat, while the white folks sat inside. "No, she wouldn't. It'll be a while before she'll be ready for that. I don't suppose she'd ever get used to that." I thought a little more. "I tell you what, Cush. If you was to ride on Regis, and I was to sit in the wagon, it'd set better with folks along the way."

He gave me a long look. "That ain't much of an improvement over the way things was, Johnny."

"We got to give it time, Cush."

"What's the war for, then?"

I sat there thinking. All along that'd been the hardest nut to crack. Pa said it was states' rights, Captain Bartlett said it was to keep the Union together, Jeb Wagner said it was to keep the darkies in their place, Cush said it was to free them. And what was it Lincoln promised in that blame speech of his? "Our forefathers brought forth a new nation dedicated to the proposition that all men are created equal"? Pa never believed blacks were the equal of whites, and Ma didn't, neither, I reckoned, except maybe in the eyes of God—their souls were just as likely to rise up to Heaven as white folks. But Lincoln, he believed it, and I reckoned a lot of folks in the North believed it, too. So maybe that was what the fighting was for, after all. "All men are created equal," I said. "Do you suppose that's it?"

"Got to be," Cush said. "It's what the Declaration promised, wasn't it?"

And what did I think? Blame me if I was

sure. For sure it is going to be a long time before kids of slaves and kids of slave owners will be able to sit together at the table of brotherhood, like the Bible says. But it was mighty hard for me to believe that Cush was lower than me. Could we still be friends? I didn't know. But I figured I'd try. "Well, Cush, you can walk home if you like, just to let everybody know you're free. But if it was me, I'd ride that mule. It's a sight more pleasant to have some company along the way."

He nodded. "There's something to that, Johnny."

How Much of This Book Is True?

The Civil War is unquestionably the most carefully studied event in American history, and we have benefited from the tremendous amount of research done on it. City Point, Petersburg, and Appomattox, and the fighting at these places was as we have described it. So, too, were the events that took place in the Shenandoah Valley, and the area where Johnny and his family lived. Generals Lee, Grant, Early, and others mentioned were historical figures and did the things we have put in the book. The same is true of Mosby and his Rangers.

Of course, Johnny, Cush, and their families are fictional. Nonetheless, they are typical of the people of their time and place, and everything that happens to them in this book did in fact happen to somebody like them.

Regrettably, the amount of killing occasioned by the Civil War was as horrifying as it appears in this book: Many more Americans died in that war than in any other. True, too, was the incredible bravery of the soldiers on both sides who went willingly to their deaths for causes they believed in.

Students interested in the Civil War will find not only a wealth of reading material to choose from but can visit many of the battlefields, which have been preserved as historic sites. The battlefields at Petersburg, Virginia, and Gettysburg, Pennsylvania, are particularly interesting, but there are many others. Readers of this book might especially enjoy a visit to Appomattox Court House.

About How People Speak in This Book

In writing a book of this kind, it is always difficult to accurately reflect the way people of an early time spoke. The truth is that people like Johnny and his family would have used a good deal of nonstandard English in their ordinary speech. Some of the other, rougher people, especially the soldiers and the teamsters we have portrayed in this book, would have used very improper English, and would have cursed regularly.

Furthermore, blacks of that time and place spoke a dialect of their own that differed in many respects from standard English. Indeed, at times it probably would be incomprehensible to us today if we heard it spoken.

In order to make this book understandable to modern readers, we have kept pretty much to standard English. However, we have scattered in some of the sort of nonstandard grammar our characters would have used; and we have added occasional touches of black dialect, just to give something of the flavor of it.

The same is true of the occasional curse words we have used. To be honest, these people would have cursed a great deal. We have occasionally employed some of the milder curse words for the sake of historical accuracy.

The Gettysburg Address
November 19, 1863
Abraham Lincoln

Four score and seven years ago our fathers brought forth on this continent, a new nation, conceived in Liberty, and dedicated to the proposition that all men are created equal.

Now we are engaged in a great civil war, testing whether that nation, or any nation so conceived and so dedicated, can long endure. We are met on a great battle-field of that war. We have come to dedicate a portion of that field, as a final resting place for those who here gave their lives that that nation might live. It is altogether fitting and proper that we should do this.

But, in a larger sense, we can not dedicate—we can not consecrate—we can not hallow—this ground. The brave men, living and dead, who struggled here, have consecrated it, far above our poor power to add or detract. The world will little note, nor long remember what we say here, but it can never forget what they did here. It is for us the living, rather, to be dedicated here to the unfinished work which they who fought here have thus far so nobly advanced. It is rather for us to be here dedicated to the great task remaining before us—that from these honored dead we take increased devotion to that cause for which they gave the last full measure of devotion—that we here highly resolve that these dead shall not have died in vain—that this nation, under God, shall have a new birth of freedom—and that government of the people, by the people, for the people, shall not perish from the earth.

JAMES LINCOLN COLLIER is the coauthor, with his brother, Christopher, of *My Brother Sam Is Dead*, a Newbery Honor Book; *The Bloody Country; The Winter Hero;* and The Arabus Trilogy: *Jump Ship to Freedom, War Comes to Willy Freeman,* and *Who Is Carrie?* Their most recent book for Delacorte is *The Clock.*

James Lincoln Collier has written many other highly acclaimed books for young readers, including *When the Stars Begin to Fall* and *The Teddy Bear Habit* and, for adults, *The Making of Jazz.* He lives in New York City.

CHRISTOPHER COLLIER is a professor of history at the University of Connecticut. His field is early American history, especially the American Revolution. He is the author of *Roger Sherman's Connecticut: Yankee Politics and the American Revolution* and other works. He and his family live in Orange, Connecticut.